Dragon Burn

Also By Donna Grant
Don't miss these other spellbinding novels!

Reaper Series
Dark Alpha's Claim
Dark Alpha's Embrace
Dark Alpha's Demand
Dark Alpha's Lover
Tall Dark Deadly Alpha Bundle

Dark King Series
Dark Heat (3 novella compilation)
Darkest Flame
Fire Rising
Burning Desire
Hot Blooded
Night's Blaze
Soul Scorched
Dragon King (novella)
Passion Ignites
Smoldering Hunger
Smoke And Fire
Dragon Fever(novella)
Firestorm
Blaze
Dragon Burn (novella)

Dark Warrior Series
Midnight's Master
Midnight's Lover
Midnight's Seduction
Midnight's Warrior
Midnight's Kiss
Midnight's Captive
Midnight's Temptation
Midnight's Promise
Midnight's Surrender (novella)

Dark Sword Series
Dangerous Highlander
Forbidden Highlander
Wicked Highlander

Untamed Highlander
Shadow Highlander
Darkest Highlander

Rogues of Scotland Series
The Craving
The Hunger
The Tempted
The Seduced

Chiasson Series
Wild Fever
Wild Dream
Wild Need
Wild Flame

LaRue Series
Moon Kissed
Moon Thrall
Moon Bound

Shield Series
A Dark Guardian
A Kind of Magic
A Dark Seduction
A Forbidden Temptation
A Warrior's Heart

Druids Glen Series
Highland Mist
Highland Nights
Highland Dawn
Highland Fires
Highland Magic
Dragonfyre (connected)

Sisters of Magic Trilogy
Shadow Magic
Echoes of Magic
Dangerous Magic

Dragon Burn

A Dark Kings Novella

By Donna Grant

1001 Dark Nights

EVIL EYE
CONCEPTS

Dragon Burn
A Dark Kings Novella
By Donna Grant

1001 Dark Nights
Copyright 2017 Donna Grant
ISBN: 978-1-945920-37-0

Foreword: Copyright 2014 M. J. Rose
Published by Evil Eye Concepts, Incorporated

Acknowledgments from the Author

A special shout out to everyone at Evil Eye who helped get this book ready, including the amazing cover. Much thanks and admiration goes Liz Berry and MJ Rose.

A special thanks Gillian and Connor for the never-ending support.

And to my readers – thank you for loving dragons!

Sign up for the 1001 Dark Nights Newsletter
and be entered to win a Tiffany Key necklace.

There's a contest every month!

Go to www.1001DarkNights.com to subscribe.

As a bonus, all subscribers will receive a free
1001 Dark Nights story
The First Night
by Lexi Blake & M.J. Rose

One Thousand and One Dark Nights

Once upon a time, in the future…

*I was a student fascinated with stories and learning.
I studied philosophy, poetry, history, the occult, and
the art and science of love and magic. I had a vast
library at my father's home and collected thousands
of volumes of fantastic tales.*

*I learned all about ancient races and bygone
times. About myths and legends and dreams of all
people through the millennium. And the more I read
the stronger my imagination grew until I discovered
that I was able to travel into the stories… to actually
become part of them.*

*I wish I could say that I listened to my teacher
and respected my gift, as I ought to have. If I had, I
would not be telling you this tale now.
But I was foolhardy and confused, showing off
with bravery.*

*One afternoon, curious about the myth of the
Arabian Nights, I traveled back to ancient Persia to
see for myself if it was true that every day Shahryar
(Persian: شـهريار, "king") married a new virgin, and then
sent yesterday's wife to be beheaded. It was written
and I had read, that by the time he met Scheherazade,
the vizier's daughter, he'd killed one thousand
women.*

Something went wrong with my efforts. I arrived in the midst of the story and somehow exchanged places with Scheherazade — a phenomena that had never occurred before and that still to this day, I cannot explain.

Now I am trapped in that ancient past. I have taken on Scheherazade's life and the only way I can protect myself and stay alive is to do what she did to protect herself and stay alive.

Every night the King calls for me and listens as I spin tales. And when the evening ends and dawn breaks, I stop at a point that leaves him breathless and yearning for more. And so the King spares my life for one more day, so that he might hear the rest of my dark tale.

As soon as I finish a story... I begin a new one... like the one that you, dear reader, have before you now.

Prologue

Before...

"You're really going through with it? With a mortal?" Sebastian asked in dismay.

Ulrik smiled and raised a mug of wine in salute. "Who am I to question love?"

Sebastian looked out over the vast rugged glen and the loch below from their perch atop a mountain on Dreagan. "What of children? None of the other humans have carried a bairn to term? Your line could die out."

"Only the cosmos knows if I'll be a father." Ulrik shrugged and took a long drink. "I'm happy. That's all I care about."

Sebastian didn't have the heart to mention that years from now, his friend might feel differently. He didn't understand why Ulrik wasn't considering every possibility, because once he was mated, that was it. He would be bound for eternity. Though, to be fair, a King didn't go through with a ceremony if there were doubts, and it was obvious Ulrik wanted the human for his mate.

Ulrik released a sigh, his gold eyes bright. "One day you'll find love, Bast. I hope I'm there to see it."

"Finding love is the least of my worries."

"Ah, that's right." Ulrik nodded, a frown forming. "So your brother is intent on marrying that young dragon?"

Sebastian drained his wine. "Aye, and that's a sore subject. Let us move to happier things. Like your mating ceremony. I hear the feast is going to be one spoken about for ages."

"It'll be the first time so many mortals, Dragon Kings, and dragons will be in one place."

"Are you worried at all?"

Ulrik laughed and placed his hand behind him, leaning back. "Why would I be? You sound like Con, always fretting about something or other. We've lived in peace for over two centuries now. My mating will be the first of many such alliances. Just wait and see."

Their peace wasn't exactly stable, but with Ulrik's euphoric state of mind he likely wouldn't recall the growing unrest of the humans or the continued displeasure of the dragons. It was something the Kings spoke about often. Only a few hours earlier Con had met with some mortals to ensure the peace continued.

As usual, Ulrik saw only the good in everything. No matter the trouble or difficulty, to Ulrik there was always a silver lining. It was one of the things Sebastian admired about his friend. And it was why Ulrik was so popular with dragons, Kings, and mortals alike.

Ulrik shook his head. "I know some of the Kings believe I should choose a dragon as my mate."

"Your pairing with a human will help the goodwill between our races."

"Everyone will soon see how blissfully content I am and realize all their worrying has been for naught." He lay back and looked at the cloudless sky. "I doona know who's more happy about my impending mating. Me or my uncle."

"Really? Your uncle?"

Ulrik laughed and said, "For once, aye."

Sebastian laughed with Ulrik. It was difficult to keep his thoughts mired in worry when his friend's cheerfulness was so infectious. "I'll always stand by your side, my friend."

"I'm lucky to have you as a friend."

He turned his head to find Ulrik holding something out to him. Sebastian reached for it to find a ring. He ran his thumb over the wide silver band with an intricate Celtic knot around it.

"I made it for you," Ulrik said.

Sebastian's head jerked up. "For me?"

There was a smile on Ulrik's face as he said, "It'll expand and shrink each time you shift so you doona have to take it off."

"Thank you." He looked back down and slid the band onto his right ring finger. Then his gaze moved back to Ulrik. "I meant it. I'll always have your back. No matter what."

Chapter One

Venice, Italy
End of January

Every decision had consequences.

Sebastian knew this better than most. His promise to Ulrik so long ago still haunted him. It was why he'd done the unthinkable and left Dreagan to find some answers on his own. The fact Constantine, the King of Dragon Kings, hadn't called to him via their mental link was worrying, but Sebastian was going to take the reprieve for however long he had it.

He strolled through the street as the cool wind buffeted him. The couples snapping pictures and selfies reminded him that Venice was a romantic destination. He gave an inward snort at the idea of romance.

What had love given Ulrik? Nothing but pain and anguish.

Sebastian checked the address as he reached the building. There was no doubt in his mind that Ryder had sent him to the right place. After all, no one at Dreagan was more adept at digging into people's lives than their resident technology expert.

The address wasn't all Ryder had given him. There was also the name of a person of interest—Gianna Santini. Along with her pertinent information.

As the personal assistant to Oscar Cox, or rather Mikkel, Gianna would know his secrets. Which was why she was Sebastian's target. And he was prepared to do anything needed to get what he was after.

It didn't matter about the vow he'd sworn as a Dragon King when the mortals appeared on this realm. His protection of them was on hold until he could help his friend. He'd let Ulrik down so long ago. Now it was his time to make up for that by proving that Ulrik wasn't responsible for everything that had happened against the Dragon Kings.

Sebastian wasn't fool enough to believe Ulrik hadn't done a few of the foul incidents, but then who could blame Ulrik after being stripped of his magic and banished from Dreagan, cursed to walk as a human, and never shift into a dragon again?

His thoughts came to a halt when Sebastian's gaze locked on his target, Gianna Santini, who walked through the glass doors of the building. Sebastian noted the black Louis Vuitton briefcase in her hand and an Yves Saint Laurent clutch in the other. She handed the briefcase to a man standing next to a black car. After a few words, she crossed the street.

He waited until the car drove away before he followed her at a slow pace. Her pale pink coat, as well as her red hair pulled back in a slick bun, was easy to spot through the dozens of people that separated them.

He wasn't sure what he'd expected, but it wasn't for her to cross a *rii*, one of the many small canals, by an ornate bridge. Almost immediately she climbed into a *topetta*.

His strides lengthened after he traversed the bridge and hailed one of the historic wooden boats for himself. He quickly handed the driver a wad of bills and said, "Private, *per favore*," as others tried to board.

The driver waved the people away and pushed out into the water. Sebastian sat, but he leaned forward, arms on his legs as he watched Gianna closely.

"Follow them," he told the driver and pointed to the *topetta* ahead of them.

The driver nodded. "*Si.*"

Not once did Gianna look behind her. Why would she? Unless she suspected she was being followed. Sebastian knew the facts about her:

-Born August 1st and raised in New York.

-Married three years to a native Italian, but divorced for five years.

-Took the job in Venice a month after her divorce.

-Was involved with several charities around Venice, but always attended the events alone.

-Never had a presence on any online dating service.

-Favorite color was pink.

-Loved opera and the ballet, based on the box she kept at both events.

-Returned to New York once a year in November for the American celebration of Thanksgiving.

-The Pomeranian she brought with her to Italy had died a year earlier.

All in all, there was nothing out of the ordinary about her. But everyone had secrets. He just had to find out what Gianna's were so he could then get the rest of the information he sought.

The man slowed and waited until Gianna disembarked from her boat before pulling up. Sebastian gave his driver a smile as he exited and pursued his target.

The edges of Gianna's coat billowed around her knees when the wind picked up. Not one hair moved out of place. She stopped before a pub and entered. Surprised, he followed her inside. The bar was upscale and obviously catered to a high-end clientele. The ultra-modern décor was just to his tastes.

While Gianna removed her jacket and sat on one of the square white stools at the bar, he opted for one of the small sofas. The place was filling up quickly with a mix of locals and tourists because of the bar's prime location next to a canal.

He ordered a whisky and let thirty minutes pass as he observed Gianna. One man approached her, and she quickly sent him away. Another tried to buy her a drink, but she declined it. A couple of others failed to get her attention.

The more Sebastian watched, the more he realized she tensed any time a man came near. It probably harkened back to her divorce. There was nothing in the facts Ryder sent him about her having a lover. A single Gianna was a much easier target.

He was going to have to make his move decisively. There could be no room for error. He had only one shot—and it had to be perfect.

The moment came when every seat but the stool on her left was taken. He rose and started toward it. His gaze landed on a man about to take it. After a brief stare down, the man quickly turned and walked the other way.

Sebastian climbed onto the stool and ignored both Gianna and the woman on the other side of him. He held his empty glass up to the bartender before setting it down.

Out of the corner of his eye, he saw Gianna look his way, so he gave her a nod in greeting, but didn't try to talk to her. Her shoulders relaxed and she went back to staring at her glass of red wine.

Through the mirror behind the bar, he studied her. It was her hair, a deep, vibrant red that drew so much attention, which went in direct contrast to the Ice Queen attitude she wore like a prize mantle.

She had flawless skin the color of cream. Red brows arched gently over large eyes the color of sparkling emeralds. Lips, wide and lusciously full, drew his gaze.

The fingers of her left hand toyed with the silver Chanel stud earrings. The white silk shirt dipped into a V at her chest and hung seductively over her breasts before tucking into a pink plaid tweed skirt. He leaned back and let his eyes travel down her shapely calves to the soft pink stilettos.

Sebastian accepted his whisky and went back to looking at her through the mirror. Gianna kept her eyes down, letting everyone know she wasn't interested in conversation. Why come to a bar then? She was a paradox, and to his delight, he discovered he wanted to peel back every layer to learn what made her tick.

It was too bad she most likely worked for the enemy, because she was someone who appeared to be interesting. Mostly because he never found a puzzle he couldn't solve. And Gianna Santini was definitely a puzzle.

Sebastian saw his chance and leaned toward her. "Can you pass me the nuts, please?"

She glanced at him before handing him the bowl. "How did you know I spoke English?"

"I took a gamble," he replied with a grin.

She didn't return his smile. When her gaze looked away, he began coming up with another way to talk to her. Then he decided on another tactic.

He tossed back his drink, laid some money on the bar, and walked out.

Chapter Two

Another long day finished with several emergencies handled. It was a specialty of hers, and one of the main reasons she'd gotten the job. Although Gianna would've done just about anything to get out of New York and begin a new life.

That's what had been offered to her in Venice. Her Italian heritage helped to ease her into living in another country. There were many things she missed about America, but she'd found a certain contentment—perhaps even happiness—in Venice.

Her first week in the city she'd found the popular bar, and she returned each evening for a drink. Most people visited such a place in order to meet others. Not her. She went because she liked the atmosphere and the view. It was nice to get a glass of wine before she headed home and did more work.

After she entered the tavern, she came to a halt when she saw the long, golden brown hair of the mystery man from the previous night sitting at the bar. He was chatting with the bartender and enjoying a whisky.

Her eyes took in the white button-down shirt that stretched tight over his wide back. His hair brushed against his shoulders as he spoke. He combed his fingers through it to shove it away from his face. She followed his hand, mesmerized, and spotted a silver ring. The previous night she'd watched the way his large hand had held the glass firmly, but at the same time gently.

Gianna blinked, realizing she'd been standing and staring. She gave her coat to a waitress before she made her way to the bar and chose a stool far from the Scot.

As her usual order was placed in front of her, she mulled over the prior night and how she'd almost asked the stranger what he was doing in Italy. His rich, deep brogue was far different than any she normally heard. It stood out, making her take notice of him.

And she wasn't the only one. There wasn't a woman in the place then—or now—who wasn't staring at him with lust and need in her eyes. Though he didn't seem to notice. He was kind to others, but didn't appear to be there to find a one-night stand.

Gianna wasn't blind to his appeal. She looked up into the mirror at him. His eyes were the first thing that drew her. They were deep and catastrophic—a vivid, lustrous golden-orange color. They shimmered with humor—and something darker, something just beneath the surface that he kept carefully hidden.

The fact she was curious about it surprised her. She couldn't remember the last time a man had intrigued her enough that she gave him a second look.

The stranger's eyes crinkled as he laughed at something. Everyone was drawn to him, hanging on his every word. He had distinct cheekbones and an angular jaw that gave him a devilishly handsome look. Strong brows arched over eyes with insanely thick lashes. His lips were wide, thin, and…seductive.

Her gaze shifted lower to his neck, where his strength could be seen in the twining cords of muscle. There was no doubt the tall stranger was appealing in so many ways that even she found herself enticed by him.

She lifted her eyes in the mirror and found him staring at her. He bowed his head, a half-smile tilting his lips. She returned his nod and lowered her gaze to her wine, embarrassed to be caught ogling him.

Gianna half expected him to move closer and attempt to talk, but he did neither. In fact, he ignored her. It was a relief.

Wasn't it?

She had no time or inclination for a dalliance of any sort. Yet she couldn't help but admit there was a slight irrational annoyance that he wasn't interested. She gave herself an inward shake. It saved her rebuffing his advances, and she was thankful for that.

Yet…the ease with which he spoke to everyone, including the bartenders, made it apparent that while she might come to the bar every night, she hadn't gotten to know anyone—or allowed them to know her.

She kept everyone at a distance, but she hadn't always been that way.

Once she finished her wine, she paid and retrieved her coat. She walked outside to find the threat of rain that had hung over them most of the day had come to fruition. The drizzle was just enough to be an irritation. Huddling within her jacket, she hurriedly made her way to the boats.

She waved her hand when she saw a *topetta* about to depart. "Wait!" she called.

But the boat was gone by the time she arrived. She turned to see if there was another when her ankle twisted and she heard something snap. She felt herself falling, pitching toward the water, and flailed her arms in an attempt to steady herself.

Suddenly, she felt strong arms grab her, yanking her up and against a hard chest. Blinking against the rain, she raised her gaze to discover the Scot's face.

He was smiling down at her. Then he said in his deep brogue, "That was a close one, lass."

She nodded, unable to find words.

"Looks like you broke a heel."

What? Her mind was too muddled to make sense of his words. Then she lifted her feet and saw one heel of her favorite Valentinos was barely hanging on. "Oh."

"Another *topetta* is coming."

She swallowed, all too aware of how her arms had instinctively gone around his neck where, even now, she clung to him. Unable to help herself, she drew in a deep breath of his woodsy scent. She should release him...but she didn't.

Topaz eyes studied her face. "Is that a dragon tattoo I see atop that lovely foot of yours?"

If there were a way for Gianna to disappear, she'd have done it. Her one and only tattoo had come the day she turned eighteen and was the first of many rebellions from her parents. It was small, but not easy to hide unless she was wearing boots.

"Yes," she admitted. To this day she had no idea why she'd chosen a dragon instead of a heart or butterfly like her friends.

"I like it," he replied with a grin. "It makes you more mysterious."

Mysterious? Her? He must be joking. She was the most boring individual alive. Wasn't that what her ex-husband used to say? She had no zeal, no enthusiasm.

No passion.

She was as dull as a rock, and she accepted that. Look where it had gotten her. She worked for one of the most influential men in the business world, and she was much more than just his assistant. She had begun running the company in Venice last year.

"And quiet too," the Scot said with a chuckle.

She lifted her shoulders in a shrug. "I apologize. It's been a long day."

"Aye, but you get to go shopping," he said, jerking his chin to the shoes.

That made her grin. "Yes, I do."

"Ah, so the idea of shopping makes you smile. I'll take note of that."

She jerked her gaze to his. Why would he care if she smiled or not? "I'm—"

"The boat is here," he said over her.

But if she thought he would set her down so she could climb aboard the *topetta* herself, she was sadly mistaken. Her hands gripped him tighter as he lightly stepped from shore onto the boat.

Once on board, he set her down before he spoke to the driver in a low tone she couldn't hear. It didn't dawn on her what had been said until they were pulling away with others still waiting.

When she looked at the Scot, he merely shrugged. She wasn't sure what to make of him. He'd been chivalrous and kind, but also charming to the point that she suspected he might be flirting. But why now? Why not at the pub?

She really should stop overanalyzing everything.

"I'm Sebastian," he said as he came to sit beside her. "Where should our driver take you?"

Sebastian. An old name that seemed to suit him. It was odd, but when she looked into his eyes she thought he was much, much older than he appeared.

He gave her a pointed look. "You still with me, lass?"

"*Sestiere Dorsoduro*," she replied.

Sebastian gave a soft whistle. "Verra nice. I doona suppose you'll give me your name since you know mine? I did save you from a dunk in the canal. That should count for something."

"Gianna. Gianna Santini," she said, unable to look away from his eyes.

His smile softened, becoming provocative and tempting. "A verra lovely name to go with a beautiful woman."

Dear God. Was that heat on her cheeks? Was she *blushing*? It had been years since anyone had made her blush.

Before she could come up with some kind of lame response, he sat back, stretching his arms along the seat, and took in Venice. It had been a while since she looked at the city like a tourist.

It was romantic and delightful, charismatic and inviting. At night, with the lights reflected off the water, it cast a quixotic spell over everything.

"I take it by your address that you live here," Sebastian said, glancing at her. "I can definitely see the appeal. It's been a considerable time since I've seen Venice, and I doona expect I'll be staying long enough this trip."

She told herself not to inquire, that she wasn't interested. Yet her lips parted and she heard herself ask, "What brings you here? Business or pleasure?"

He turned his head to her. "I'm beginning to think a wee bit of both."

Dammit. She was blushing again. What was it about him that affected her so? She didn't like it. At all. It had to stop.

Sebastian drew in a deep breath and slowly released it. "If you doona mind me asking, how long have you lived here? I heard you speak fluent Italian, but I can hear your American accent."

"I spend so much of my time speaking Italian that sometimes I forget," she admitted with a small laugh. "I've been here five years. Sometimes it feels like I've been here forever, and other times like I just arrived."

Now why the hell did she tell him that?

He nodded slowly. "I've felt that way a few times myself. Even so, Venice seems to suit you."

"It's my home. And you? Do you live in Scotland?"

"Aye," he replied with a wide smile. A wistfulness came over his face. "There's nowhere else I'd rather be."

She couldn't imagine feeling like that about a place. To love something so deeply it showed in his eyes and through his voice. "Then

I hope your business doesn't keep you away for long."

"I'm sure it willna." He stretched his legs out as the boat ambled along. "Have you ever been to Scotland?"

"I can't say that I have. The closest I've been was a three-day trip to London."

He quirked a brow. "When was that?"

"Oh," she said, thinking back. "It's been about four years."

"Tell me you went there for a holiday?" he implored.

She found herself grinning again. "Business."

He twisted his lips ruefully. "Well, in all honesty, you didna miss much. Now if you really want to see history and the untamed, rugged countryside, then you need to visit the Highlands."

"I'll make note of that."

The boat slowed and she realized they had reached her neighborhood. She'd been having such a pleasant time that it went by entirely too quickly. In fact, she was almost sorry the night was coming to an end. It was the best time she'd had in…well, a long, long time.

Despite the nice evening, she didn't know Sebastian—or trust him. She took the driver within two blocks of her house and had him pull over.

Sebastian exited the boat and held out his hand to help her. She took it, meeting his gaze as she disembarked. Once on solid ground, she reluctantly withdrew from his grip.

"If you're no' busy, we could take a ride around Venice," he offered.

The fact she seriously considered it was another shock. "I've got a long day tomorrow."

"You work on the weekend?"

"I work all the time."

He leaned his head to the side and regarded her. "Life is short, lass. You should have some fun every now and again."

"You're implying that I don't?"

He shrugged as he raised a brow. "You're the one who said you work all the time."

So she had.

"You intrigue me, Gianna Santini. A beautiful woman who sits at a bar drinking red wine alone and works all the time. It's a shame to waste such a life."

"I—"

"Doona say anything," he said over her. "I'm going to be at the Piazza San Marco tomorrow morning before visiting the Doge's Palace. Forget your work for a day. Come spend it with me. I'll make it a day you willna forget."

He lifted her hand and kissed the back of it before returning to the boat. There he stood, watching her as it drove away.

All the while, his offer rang in her head.

Chapter Three

Sebastian walked the Piazza San Marco while drinking his coffee. He stared at the two columns where capital executions used to take place. Mortals could be a brutal, fierce race.

He slowly moved his eyes around him, watching the tourists clicking pictures from their mobile phones with the columns in the background as if the gruesome history didn't affect them.

After Gianna left him the night before, he'd returned to the palazzo, one of the many residences owned by Dreagan, confident in his plan of seduction for Gianna. But the longer it went without any communication from Con, the more concerned Sebastian became. He could plead his case, but he knew all too well just how Con felt about Ulrik.

Until Sebastian had the proof in hand that he knew was out there, he wouldn't bother talking to Con. It was the right decision, he knew it. Despite that, he had a disconnect from Dreagan because of it, and it left him feeling exposed.

A sensation he hadn't experienced since the war with the humans.

He threw away his empty cup and turned, only to still when his gaze landed on Gianna. He slowly smiled because his toughest hurdle had been cleared.

He'd gotten the elusive and frigid mortal to put aside her work and join him. Now that she was with him, he was going to make sure she never wanted to leave. What he was doing to Gianna was shite. He didn't want to put her in the middle of things, but it was his only way to help Ulrik.

For several seconds they stared at each other, the people milling about between them unseen and unheard. He made his way to Gianna through a mass of pigeons that took to the skies as he approached.

He looked her over in approval. The camel-colored pants sculpted to her long, lean legs and showed off her very shapely bum. A simple black sweater could be seen beneath her belted black coat with its wide collar. Tall black riding boots and a black handbag draped over one shoulder completed the outfit.

Her long red tresses were once more pulled away from her face in a bun. And he was dying to loosen it to see just how long her hair was.

But that would come later.

Right after he kissed her.

"Good morning," he said.

She moved her hand behind her ear as if tucking hair, her finger brushing against the large, round, rose gold stud earring. Her gaze lowered to the ground for a heartbeat before returning to his face. "Good morning."

"I didna think you'd come."

She took a deep breath, her lips softening as she said, "I hadn't intended to."

"But here you are."

"Here I am."

He smiled, feeling confident in his plans. "Would you like some coffee?"

"I would, thanks."

They strolled side by side to a café. There he seated her before taking his own chair. He wanted her to grow accustomed to him so he could begin putting the difficult questions to her. Rushing would only set him back where he'd started. Patience was what was needed now.

After they ordered, she sat back, staring at him. There was no nervous hand wringing or refusing to meet his gaze. The woman across from him didn't appear to be afraid of anything. Though he'd like to see how she reacted to him in his true form.

"Why are you smiling?" she asked.

He moved his hand in an arc. "Look around. This place is beautiful. Does it no' make you want to smile?"

"You look at the world as if you've lived a charmed life where nothing has gone wrong."

It took a lot for him to keep the grin in place at her words. "On the contrary, I've had my share of unfortunate and tragic events."

"And still you smile?"

"Nothing will change the past. What's done is done. I could walk around with a frown in place, but what does that give me? Nothing but misery."

She crossed one leg over the other. "So you're an optimist."

"If choosing to be happy makes me an optimist, then aye. I suppose I am. Are you a pessimist?"

"A realist," she replied succinctly.

Their coffee arrived. When she sat up to pour cream in it, he asked, "What does a realist see?"

She looked up with startled green eyes. "What do I see?"

"Aye, lass. I look around and see beauty, even romance. I see couples celebrating honeymoons, anniversaries, or just their love. I see kids staring in wonder at the sights, and couples holding hands."

She held her cup between her hands and sat back once more. "That's very optimistic of you."

"You doona see the same?"

"Oh, I see the beauty and the romance. I see exhausted parents, fighting siblings, and couples hoping a trip would rekindle whatever it was they lost, whenever they lost it."

He sipped his coffee and regarded her with curiosity. "That sounds like you're tipping into the pessimistic side."

To his surprise, she smiled briefly. "I think I was."

"What could make a stunning woman like yourself so cynical?"

"I'm just lucky I guess."

It was going to take much more to open her up. For the majority of the mortals, it took only a small nudge to get them to talk about themselves. Gianna was the exception. Not only was she malcontent and a loner, but she was fiercely independent and exceedingly private.

Which, surprisingly, made him want to know her even more. Again, she reminded him she was a puzzle. And he was very good at solving those.

"What about you?" she asked. "What makes you so sanguine?"

"That's a long story."

She raised a red brow. "Afraid to tell it?"

Her taunt made him laugh. If she only knew...

"I've a friend who has been going through a verra difficult time for what feels like an eternity, but I think I've figured out a way to help him."

She raised her cup to him. "Bravo. You must be a good friend indeed to take time out of your life to help him."

"Would you no' do the same?"

"If I had friends, yes."

Her confession, given as if it meant nothing, mystified him. It was a natural course of almost every being to have at least one person they could turn to. Gianna had pushed everyone away, even moving far from her family.

He realized there might be an opportunity for him now. "I have a large family. My friend is really like a brother. I'll do anything for my family."

"So you're close to them?"

"Aye," he said with a nod.

The sound of a child's laughter caught her attention. She turned her head to watch a couple with three young children walk past. "I only see my family once a year."

"Do you miss them?"

"I was really close to my mother. More so than was probably normal for a mother-daughter relationship. She was my best friend, the one person I turned to for everything. She died seven years ago."

That was information Ryder hadn't given him. Probably because he didn't think it was pertinent to the mission. "I'm verra sorry."

"She was the glue that held our family together." Gianna smiled softly. "She was very optimistic, just like you. But," Gianna said, the light fading from her eyes. "When she was gone, there was no one to buffer my father and me."

Sebastian took another drink of coffee. "Family can be a blessing as well as a curse."

"No truer words have been spoken."

"So you find happiness in your work?"

She sat up a little straighter and leaned forward, setting her cup on the table, but continuing to keep her hands around it. "Most people work in order to live. I live to work. It brings me fulfillment."

"You're good at what you do then?"

"I am."

He liked her confidence as well as her ability to admit her strengths without sounding vain or arrogant. She seemed tightly wound, just like her hair. And he was ready to loosen her up—and make her burn. He hadn't expected to feel such...hunger...for her, but there was no denying it was there.

"What is it that you do, exactly?" he asked.

Her face lit up as she spoke of recently taking control of a multibillion-dollar business. "But that's just in the past year. My main job is that of personal assistant to Oscar Cox. He's a British businessman who has made his wealth in various companies."

"Why Venice?" he asked. "Could you no' find a job like this in New York?"

She set aside her finished mug and gave a slight shrug. "I was on my way to having such a position in New York, but I wanted a fresh start. It turns out my uncle had a friend in Venice who told him about the job. He urged me to apply for it. I intended to, but before I could, a headhunter called me about the position. The next thing I knew, I had a phone interview, then I was flying to Italy for a face-to-face interview. I got the post a week later."

"Sounds like it was meant to be." It also sounded as if her family might have a connection to Mikkel, who was posing as Oscar Cox. "What do you do, exactly, as a personal assistant?"

"Everything," she said with a chuckle. "I keep his calendar in order, schedule meetings, plan events, correspond with individuals, make his travel arrangements, and things like that."

"I see."

It would be so much easier if Sebastian didn't have to hide everything from Gianna. The problem was, he needed to determine if the man who owned her company and committed various crimes against the Dragon Kings was Mikkel and not Ulrik before he could take the next step.

He knew in his gut it wasn't Ulrik. Not that Ulrik was innocent of everything. But Con saw their old friend in a different light because he had no choice. Sebastian wasn't confined by the restrictions placed upon Con by being the King of Dragon Kings. That allowed Sebastian more freedom, and it gave him the ability to look for things that might just verify what he knew to be fact—that the Mikkel everyone at Dreagan kept hearing about was in fact someone other than Ulrik.

The fact Mikkel and Ulrik looked nearly like twins was what made Sebastian keep coming back to them being family. That and a distant memory of Ulrik having an uncle named Mikkel. It couldn't be a coincidence. Did that mean that Ulrik knew about Mikkel? If so, why were they working together?

The obvious answer was that Mikkel wanted to be a Dragon King. Which wasn't going to happen as long as Ulrik was alive.

That realization went through Sebastian like dragon fire. He looked around, his mind racing. If Mikkel was after Ulrik's position, then that meant he had some way to kill Ulrik.

"Sebastian?"

He jerked his head and attention back to Gianna. "Aye?"

"Are you all right? Because you looked like you remembered something awful," she said, concern clouding her gaze.

He made his shoulders relax as he smiled. "My apologies. The business that brought me here intruded for a moment."

"Perhaps I can help."

"Aye, but let's discuss that later. I'm ready to see Doge's Palace. Will you come with me?"

She uncrossed her legs, her lips curving in a smile. "I think I will."

Sebastian paid their bill and they rose together. He put his hand on the small of her back as he guided her through the tables. He saw the way her head turned to the side and her eyes lowered to his arm.

He gazed down at her as she looked forward, her chin lifted. The more time he spent with her, the more she captivated and fascinated him, which made his job of seducing her even easier.

His eyes traveled to her mouth. Every time she spoke, his gaze would drift to her full lips. His balls tightened each time there was even the slightest curve to her mouth. And when she'd blushed last night, he'd hardened.

She was an Ice Queen begging to be thawed.

And he was just the Dragon King to do it.

Chapter Four

Seduction can come upon you like a whisper, brushing against your skin with a subtle promise. It can surround you like warm velvet, its caress provocative and tempting. It can blitz you, overwhelming your senses until there is only one thought—him.

Gianna didn't know when, she didn't know how, but Sebastian's seduction had flooded her like the wispy fingers of mist before effortlessly besieging with the skill of a warlord.

Ever since she found herself in his arms the night before, she hadn't been able to get him out of her mind. Not even work could shove him aside.

She'd passed the night weighing his offer of spending the day with him. She waffled back and forth until she finally dozed off. When she woke and got into the shower, she still hadn't come to a decision.

As she'd left her home that morning, she'd told herself she was going for coffee. And ended up at the Piazza San Marco.

With him.

She'd seen him long before he noticed her. It gave her a chance to study him at leisure. He wore black slacks and a button-down in a purple so deep in color it was almost black. The black leather jacket sat upon his wide shoulders like an afterthought instead of a necessity.

The breeze was gentle, ruffling the ends of his golden brown hair that swept atop his shoulders. He studied the architecture around him, not with wonder, but...almost as if it was intruding.

Not once did he appear to notice any of the women who endeavored to capture his attention. Yet he looked down and smiled at the pigeons who came close to him. And he gazed at children with a kind of amazement, like he wasn't sure what to think of them, but he couldn't look away.

Like she couldn't stop staring at him.

Then he turned and locked eyes with her. Her heart had actually tripped over itself. Not once in her life had she ever experienced such a reaction to anything. Chills raced over her body that had nothing to do with the cool temperatures and everything to do with the enigmatic, baffling man who held her utterly spellbound.

His smile was both sensual and secretive. She didn't remember what he said after he walked to her. It had been a question, and she'd agreed. The next thing she knew, they were having coffee.

To say she was shocked to find herself talking so readily to him was an understatement. What was it about him that made her feel comfortable? Relaxed, even?

As they walked from the café, his hand rested on the small of her back. The pressure of his palm against her was so profound that, for a moment, she wondered if she had on clothes, because it felt as if he were touching her skin.

Once the mass of people thinned out, he dropped his arm to his side. Gianna's displeasure at that set her on edge. Nothing was as it should be. It was as if she was being spun this way and that, turned upside down, and just before landing on her feet, she was twirled about again.

As they approached the Doge's Palace, she saw none of the grandeur, despite it being one of her favorite museums. Because today every fiber was attuned to the man standing at her side.

Once inside, she barely looked at the ornate canvases and frescoes by some of Venice's greatest artists or any of the magnificent Venetian Gothic style architecture that made the palace into such a tourist draw.

It wasn't until they walked into the sumptuously decorated Chamber of the Great Council that she took notice. He stopped them in the middle of the room to take it all in.

"The world's longest canvas painting," he said as he looked at the *Paradiso* that was painted above the Doge's throne.

She met his gaze. "In one of the largest rooms in all of Europe." Gianna then motioned to the work ringing the top of the walls. "The same artist, Jacopo Tintoretto, also painted the portraits of all the past doges in order."

Sebastian walked to the section where a black cloth was painted in place of a portrait. "Ah, the infamous Doge Marin Faliero. His face would've been here had he no' committed the ultimate treason."

"Unfortunately for him, his coup attempt failed, which resulted in his death as well as the *damnatoio memoriae*," she said.

"Total eradication of his name and memory from all records."

She frowned when she saw grief fill Sebastian's eyes, and she knew it had nothing to do with Faliero. When he caught her looking, he wiped away any trace of sadness.

It appeared that the optimist had something dark in his past. Or perhaps it was his present. She had a suspicion that somehow that was what brought him to Venice. It was on the tip of her tongue to ask, but she held back at the last minute.

Whatever he was involved in didn't include her, and she needed to keep it that way. No matter how sexy he might be, Sebastian was just a minor diversion she was allowing herself.

And nothing more.

"Come," he said as they walked through another set of doors when a tour guide called for them.

Their fingers brushed, causing something hot and charged to ignite through her veins. She was so distracted by her reaction that it took her a second to realize he had bought the Secret Itineraries tour, which allowed them to visit the tiny offices that wrapped around the palace through corridors paved with wooden planks and ceilings so low Sebastian had to bend not to hit his head.

Excitement flared within her when the guide spoke of the various entrances to the offices hidden behind secret doors set into oil paintings and carved woodwork. With every minute taking in the grandeur and history, Gianna was regretting spending all her time working and not getting out to see more of Venice during her years there. How sad that she'd missed such beauty.

"This thrills you," Sebastian whispered.

She smiled up at him and nodded. "The old world intrigues me. The idea of private secretaries keeping records of accusations made against both the rich and the poor is incredible."

"A world you'd want to be part of?"

"Definitely not. I don't think I'd survive it."

His topaz gaze intensified. "I doona think you give yourself credit."

She didn't have a chance to reply as the small tour group moved onward. His hand found the small of her back again, and she discovered she had no wish to push him away. His touch was...soothing.

He moved close as their guide took them through secret passages to a large chamber where the Council of Ten met to decide the fate of the Republic as well as the people who crossed them.

It was while they were walking from one secret doorway into another that she found herself inside the inquisition room, where a hangman's rope still dangled, as if waiting to dispense justice. Sebastian's arm wound around her, moving her aside as a woman brushed roughly past.

Gianna glared at the woman who didn't apologize. Then she felt the heat radiating from Sebastian's chest as she was plastered against him. A slow burn began inside her, one that took her a second to comprehend what it was—desire. She shoved it aside and moved out of his arms.

She half-listened to the rest of the tour since she was focused on every sound, every movement Sebastian made. When he came too near, she hoped he didn't touch her.

Then she prayed that he would.

When their tour concluded, she was wondering how to end her time with him. She wasn't sure she could handle any more of the desire that continued to build at a rapid rate.

She walked out of the palace and straight to the balcony overlooking the water. When she turned to tell him she was leaving, he stood mere inches from her. She stood frozen as he reached up and gently smoothed his thumb across her cheekbone.

Her heart thrummed against her ribs as blood pounded in her ears. Topaz eyes watched her intently. She gave a half-hearted attempt to look away, but she succeeded only in blinking.

There was something magnetic about Sebastian, some kind of allure that made him irresistible. She battled an uncontrollable urge to lean into him and allow her passion to flow freely.

He shifted his gaze to his thumb, which he held between them. Her eyes lowered to his lips as she imagined what it might feel like to kiss him. Her blood heated at the thought.

The desire was so strong that she had to tear her eyes from his mouth. She glanced to his thumb, where she saw an eyelash right before the wind swept it away. Unable to help herself, she looked into his face, their gazes tangling.

He leaned forward slowly, and her heart literally tripped over itself. She held her breath, her lids falling shut as he neared.

Then she heard his husky brogue next to her ear. "Doona leave. The day is just getting started."

Dear God. How could she refuse that sexy voice? Did he know it was a weapon? Because he expertly used it in such a way that she was aching for him.

"Gianna."

He had to stop talking. She couldn't take any more.

"Stay," he urged.

Every argument she had to return home vanished as if they'd never existed. She licked her dry lips and opened her eyes against the bright sunlight just as he was straightening.

He raised a brow in question, and she found herself nodding. She was able to relax when he took a step back, but that didn't last for long as the crowds forced them to walk so that they were constantly touching in some way.

It was a drain on her senses. Every touch sent her spinning into an abyss of desire, one she fought—or she tried to. If those casual contacts were torture, it was his intentional ones that drove her to the edge of reason. There was always a valid cause for his touch. Her eyelash, a family walking past, or dodging someone.

They meandered slowly through the streets despite the quick pace of others. The world around them vibrated with sound while they remained silent. She glanced at him, taking in his profile. His face was solemn, his eyes held a faraway look. But if she thought his mind was elsewhere, she was proven wrong the next minute when he quickly turned her away from a set of rowdy teenagers.

How did she keep ending up in his arms? It almost felt like it was destiny showing her her path. But Gianna wanted to reject it. She'd proved once before that she needed only her job. She could—and would—do it again. Having a lover was nice, but she didn't need one.

"It's a good thing I'm with you," Sebastian said with a grin. "That's the second time I've saved you from a collision."

"So it seems."

A small frown puckered his brow. "What is going on in that mind of yours, Gianna Santini?"

"Why did you ask me to come with you today?" Now that the question was out, she had to know the answer. Because she wasn't at all sure about the emotions colliding within her. She stepped out of his arms and held his gaze.

His smile remained in place, but his eyes grew shrewd. "I didna want to spend the day alone."

"Yes, but why me? Why not any of the other women in that bar who didn't take their eyes off you?"

"Perhaps because you were no' staring at me."

She should've seen that coming. "So you think I'm playing hard to get?"

"I doona think you're playing, but that didna have anything to do with why I asked you to join me today. And why you accepted."

As if she was going to let him say something like that and not see what he meant. "So why did you ask me?"

Before, his responses had been quick. Now he swallowed and let the silence stretch between them. She was beginning to think that she wasn't going to like his answer, and that disappointed her.

He disappointed her.

"I saw something in you," he finally said. "You go to that bar and drink alone, never engaging with anyone else. Then you return to your home, only to repeat the same scene again."

"So you think my life is sad?" Her defenses immediately went up, ready to do battle.

"I think you need something in your life. I know this because I'm missing something in mine."

She wasn't prepared for that explanation. In fact, it set her aback. Every time he spoke, she wanted to know more about him. "What are you missing?"

"My friend. My brother. I need to get him back home."

Chapter Five

Truth was always better than a lie, no matter the basis. It was the reason Sebastian decided to tell Gianna part of the facts.

Her green eyes were inquisitive as she searched his face. When she accepted his response, she gave a small nod. "You're here for your friend."

"I am."

"Is he missing?"

Sebastian briefly looked to the side and the people that moved around and between them. "No' exactly."

"What exactly, then?"

He pressed his lips together as he felt constrained by those around him. The more he tried to ignore the mortals, the more he was aware of them. It was a reminder of how they could move freely about, but he couldn't—not as a dragon.

His human form felt like a cage, a prison that he couldn't break out of. His vow to protect the mortals was his shackles, keeping him grounded and forever yearning for the sky.

"Come," he heard her say over the roar in his head.

Her fingers slipped into his as she tugged him after her. After several steps, he found himself looking at their joined hands. He'd been slowly seducing her all day, noticing how she tried to keep distance between them while he maneuvered them into situations that brought them closer together.

And yet, she was the one who took his hand. That simple deed had a profound effect on him. She had seen him upset and reacted without guile or pretense.

It made him very aware that he was intentionally deceiving her. Even though he had a good excuse, it was still wrong. Yet there was no other way. He knew facts about her, but he didn't know *her*.

Not that it would make a difference in what he told her of Ulrik or the Dragon Kings. Regardless if she was working with Mikkel or not, Sebastian would leave her with no knowledge that could harm his brethren.

It was something none of the other Kings had been able to accomplish, but he had a plan—a foolproof plan that would earn him the evidence about Mikkel and keep Gianna unaware of the Dragon Kings.

To his surprise—and pleasure—she took them to a dock and climbed aboard a gondola.

Once she was seated, she looked up at him and rolled her eyes. "Not a word. You looked like you needed some privacy, and I'm giving it to you."

"We could've had privacy at my home."

At this, she smiled. "This is better."

He knew for a fact it wasn't, but he was willing to go for the romantic ride on the famous Venetian boats if she was. Sebastian stepped into the boat and sat beside her.

In no time, they were gliding across the water. He took a deep breath, feeling better now that he was away from the narrow walkways and crowds of people.

"Tell me about your friend," she pressed.

He turned his head to her. "Why are you so interested?"

"I shouldn't be, but I am. I know this city. Perhaps I can help."

That's exactly what he wanted to hear her say. "It's no' without risks."

"You should see some of the businesses and people I deal with. I can handle it," she told him. "Why don't you start by telling me his name?"

"Ulrik."

"Ulrik what? Does he have a surname?"

Sebastian shrugged. "He changes it, so it doesna matter."

"That's going to make finding him difficult."

"As I said, he's no' really missing."

She folded her hands in her lap. "I think I'm confused. You're looking for him, but he's not missing?"

"He had a heated disagreement with our...brother, Con. Words were exchanged, and he was sent away." It was the basics of the story, but hopefully enough to give Gianna the answers she sought.

"How long ago?"

"Awhile. Things need to be sorted between Ulrik and Con."

She looked out over the water. "Sometimes it's better not to force things."

"They used to be inseparable."

"What makes you think Ulrik is in Venice?"

"He's no'."

Her forehead puckered. "I don't understand. You said he was missing."

"He is."

"But he isn't in Venice?"

Sebastian shook his head.

She let out a sigh. "But you came here because of Ulrik."

"I'm looking for a man who could go a long way in sorting out the nastiness between Ulrik and Con."

"Ah," she said with a nod. "I see. And do you know who this man is?"

"I have a suspicion."

"A name?" she asked.

He stretched his legs out in front of him and crossed them at the ankle. "No' really."

"Then how do you know he's in the city?"

"He has dealings in Venice. I'm hoping I catch him here."

She leaned her head back. "That's quite a story. Is it true?"

"Aye."

"Have you thought of hiring a private investigator?"

"Briefly."

She raised her brows and looked his way. "You'd rather do this on your own?"

"I have to."

"You seem like that type of man."

That made him smile. "I'm a type?"

"Yes," she said with a small laugh.

"What type, exactly?"

She shrugged and looked skyward before she said, "The type who sets off to another country to find a man who could right the wrong done to his friend. The kind of man who saves a stranger and asks her to sightsee with him the next day. The kind of man who sits in a bar with everyone hanging on his every word. The kind of man who doesn't seem to notice or care about all the women fawning over him."

"You were no' hanging on my every word or fawning over me," he pointed out. To his delight, her cheeks turned pink, a dead giveaway that she had been listening to him at the bar.

"Everyone else was."

He found he liked when she blushed. It was...endearing. "Where do you get your red hair?"

"My mother's side. I believe there were some Scots ancestors."

"Lass," he said in mock offence. "You have Scots blood and you've never visited Scotland? I doona know what to think."

She laughed, shaking her head at him. "I've been busy."

"But have you been living your own life?"

Her lips parted as she began to answer, then she hesitated. "I thought I was. It wasn't until just now that I remembered making a list when I was in college of all the places I wanted to visit. I haven't thought of that list in years."

"Sometimes it takes someone forcing you out of your daily routine to see what you've been missing."

She cut her eyes to him. "You're saying I need to get out more?"

"Aye," he said with a firm nod.

She bit her bottom lip as she let out a deep breath. "I'm in Europe and not taking the opportunity to travel. Rome is not that far. Neither are the Alps. Greece. Nice. Berlin. I do need to make another list and actually start traveling."

He was enamored with her enthusiasm. The Ice Queen did have passion. It only needed to be brought to the surface. And she needed to be reminded of it.

Sebastian wanted to reach over and take her hand, to pull her against him and place his lips against hers. Not because he was wooing her, but because it seemed like that's what he should do.

If he didn't know better, he'd begin to suspect that Gianna was seducing him. An Ice Queen would never do that.

Would she?

She looked at him with her clear, green gaze. "Have you ever forgotten something you once wanted to do?"

He thought back to a time before the war with the mortals, when dragons still filled the skies. He'd been thinking of his own future, his own children, when Ulrik was getting ready to be mated. Sebastian never considered a mortal for his mate because he wanted to continue his family line. He'd always known he wanted kids. As many as he could have.

Though that was never to be.

"I'm sorry."

Gianna's soft voice reached him. He slid his gaze to her and found her eyes filled with remorse.

"I made you think of something sad," she said. "That wasn't my intention."

He saw her turning her stud earring and reached up to gently tug her hand away. "The past can no' be hidden for long. It always shows itself, most times when you least expect it."

"The past can be buried."

"No' for long. Trust me."

Her head tilted as she studied him. "I look into your eyes and it's like I'm looking through eternity. It's as if you see the world differently than the rest of us."

He almost found himself admitting that he did, but he held his tongue.

"Old eyes," she said. "That's what you have. My mother used to say that you could tell a lot about a person from their eyes. I never understood her saying until now. What have you seen?"

"Too much."

Her fingers brushed against his cheek as she stroked down his face. "You've seen death."

"Aye," he whispered, drawn to answer in a way he could neither explain nor understand.

"Destruction and the end of..." She blinked, confusion contorting her face. "Something important."

He put his hand over hers and gently lowered it. "What else do you see?"

"Pain and...hope," she said with a smile.

Hope? She must have that wrong. The only kernel of hope inside him was finding Mikkel in order to get Ulrik back to Dreagan where he belonged.

He gradually leaned closer, lured to her by an invisible force he couldn't seem to shake. "I have little hope."

"You're an optimist though."

"Perhaps I'm a realist."

She shook her head, her lips coming closer. Her eyes softened, blinking slowly. "If I asked you who you really were, would you answer?"

"You wouldna believe me."

"But would you tell me?"

It was with regret that he said, "There's nothing to tell, lass. I'm simply a man."

"Your eyes say something quite different."

Even hearing her say that, he couldn't look away. It was almost as if he wanted her to see the dragon within, to see him in his true form—and accept him.

"Who are you?" she whispered as her eyes closed.

He caressed along her jaw, her head leaning back so he could reach her neck. He was captivated by her plump lips, which were parted and waiting for his kiss.

She had seen a part of him that he kept tightly sealed away, a part that he refused to think about. With one question, she had brought all those old feelings and wishes to the surface. He should be angry, but all he felt was a raging desire that was burning him from the inside out.

He closed the distance between them to kiss her when the gondolier announced the ride was over.

Chapter Six

Gianna walked away from the gondola as if in a dream. Her body felt lethargic, weighed down by the passion that had been steadily and skillfully stroked.

He was there, beside her. His warmth infusing her, his nearness making her burn. The pressure of his splayed hand on her back sent heat rushing through her veins. She wanted to feel him against her skin, to have his weight atop her as their bodies rubbed together.

She couldn't remember the last time she felt so wanton, so uninhibited.

So...shameless.

What had happened on the gondola ride? She couldn't help but believe that something had occurred and she'd missed it. As if in their shared conversation, some hidden doorway had been opened and she'd willingly—happily, even—walked through it.

Now, as she stood inside, she was disoriented and unsettled. Anxious and dazed. She wanted to reach out for something to hold onto. It was only then she realized that whatever doorway she'd walked through, she hadn't gone alone.

Sebastian was there.

She turned her head to look at him. He met her gaze, his clear eyes holding some kind of emotion she couldn't quite name, but through it she saw the fires of desire as if he were lit from the inside with them.

It caused her stomach to flutter in excitement and her feet to stop working. She stumbled, which caused his arm to wrap around her waist as he drew to a stop and hauled her against him. They stared silently into each other's eyes as the crowds parted and walked around them. The steady thumping of his heartbeat could be felt beneath her palms.

What was it about Sebastian that made her forget herself? She was a different person with him, one that not only enjoyed his touch—but craved it.

The problem was, she liked how she felt around him. She enjoyed how he made her feel, and how she *wanted* to feel. The desire, the need, the hunger. She reached for it, accepted it.

Embraced it.

She didn't know how long they stood there lost in each other's eyes. For a brief moment, she wondered if it was one-sided. Could Sebastian feel the same as her? Did she dare allow herself to follow wherever this road led, no matter how many doorways she walked through?

No matter what it might expose within herself?

No matter what longing it might reveal?

No matter if she found herself walking alone?

She was standing on the edge of a precipice while he stood on nothing but air, holding out his hand and urging her to jump. Never one to take such a chance, she found herself wanting to do just that.

Even if it meant that she could hit the ground so hard she might never get up again.

It was strange to even consider any of this. Yet here she was. There should be more fear, more concern. Perhaps it was the desire overshadowing those other emotions.

"Gianna," he began.

Her cell phone vibrated in her purse, causing her to jump and shattering whatever had held them enthralled. She couldn't help but wonder if destiny was trying to tell her something. It was the second time they'd been interrupted that day when she'd felt sure he was going to kiss her.

By the vibration tone, it was her boss calling. "I'm sorry," she said as she stepped back and pulled out her cell. Then she turned away and walked to the side of the street to answer it. "Hello, sir."

"Is everything in order for tonight?"

She inwardly winced at Oscar's brusque tone. Not that he was exactly a friendly person, but it was never a good sign when he was angry. And by the clipped tone of his British accent, he was bordering on livid. "Yes, sir."

"Are you sure?" he demanded.

She enjoyed her job. It was taxing and trying at times, but it paid very well and gave her a measure of freedom she couldn't get anywhere else. "I'm certain of it."

There was a long, tense stretch of silence. Then he said, "Since when do you plan one of my parties and not be there to oversee every detail?"

"I've trained my people well. If there's a problem, they would've reached out to me."

"This is very unlike you, Gianna. What are you doing?" His tone suddenly changed. It was smooth, soft. Coaxing.

She was immediately on edge. "I took some time to myself."

"Today? Of all days?"

"Everything will be perfect tonight. I promise," she stated, unnerved by his call and his words.

"It better."

The line disconnected. She lowered the phone and looked at the ground. Her day with Sebastian was over, and she was angry about it.

"What is it?" Sebastian asked as he came to stand beside her.

She faced him, regret souring her stomach. "Thank you for a lovely morning."

"It's no' even noon yet," he said with a frown.

"I know. Unfortunately, my boss needs me."

Sebastian quirked a brow. "On a Saturday?"

"When you're a personal assistant, you work when they work."

"Do you no' get any days off?"

She tucked her cell phone back in her purse. "I do, but today isn't one of them."

"What's so important about today?"

"He's hosting a masquerade ball tonight. The guests are a select group of people he's done business with, and others he's cultivating a business relationship with. These are VIPs in the truest since of the word. And everything has to be perfect."

Disappointment filled his eyes. "Then I shall keep you no more."

His acceptance of it only made her want to stay more. It was the first time since she began working for Oscar Cox that she wanted to tell her boss no. But she never would.

She started to tell Sebastian she'd had a great time and realized she'd already said that. Then she debated asking him if they could see each other again, but something held her back. She wasn't sure what it was.

He took her hand in his and rubbed his thumb along the back. "Come find me when you're finished."

"I—"

"No matter the time or how many days have passed," he interrupted her.

She was having a hard time holding back a smile. "I don't know how."

"Did I no' tell you?" he asked with a sexy half-grin. "I live in San Polo. It's the palazzo directly opposite the Town Hall palace."

Her mouth fell open as she realized he was talking about the famed 17th century palazzo that had both front and side views of the Grand Canal. The very home her boss had tried unsuccessfully to acquire for himself—three times.

Just what family did Sebastian come from?

"Have a good day, Gianna," he said as he bent and kissed her hand. Then he looked up at her and declared, "And know I'll be thinking of you."

She could only watch as he straightened and walked away. It took her several minutes to get control of herself after she lost sight of him when he turned the corner.

With a loud sigh, she pivoted and started toward Oscar's house— also on the Grand Canal. The entire walk, she couldn't stop thinking about Sebastian. Even once she was inside the palazzo and checking each room to ensure the flowers were right before stopping to chat with the caterer and then the decorator, Sebastian was always there, just at the fringes of her mind.

As she stood back and watched the final touches go up, she thought about the evening to come. Her gown had arrived weeks ago with the matching mask. Her only duties that night were to be on standby in case of an emergency, which there never was.

When she thought of all the balls and parties her employer had hosted, not one of them had she attended with an escort. Yet she'd never felt more clearly alone than she did now. And she didn't like it. Perhaps it was time to turn another page in her life and rethink what she wanted. No longer was it so important for her to be alone.

What infuriated her was that she couldn't remember why that had been so important in the first place.

She wanted Sebastian with her. His departing remarks led her to believe that he was interested in seeing her again. Perhaps it was time she stopped standing on the sidelines. Maybe this new door she'd walked through was a wakeup call to actually take a chance.

Gianna pulled out her phone and made a quick call before she was summoned to make some changes to the guest list. Her eyes scanned the names. Over a hundred people from all across the globe were attending. Only four had declined, with two more having to cancel at the last minute.

With each hour that grew closer to the time for her to begin getting ready, she found she was nervous and eager. When she could take it no more, she ducked out and hurried home to begin dressing.

She had never taken so long in the shower before, lathering her hair and body twice. Once she was dried off and her hair combed, she took special care to rub lotion over her entire body. Every place she touched, she imagined it was Sebastian's hands on her. Her desire intensified, spreading and multiplying as it expanded.

Slipping into her pink silk robe, she sat before her vanity and stared at her reflection for long minutes. The woman looking back at her was different. It couldn't be seen on the outside, but inside, everything had been rearranged. She wanted to look as different as she felt.

No. She *needed* to look different to match what was changing inside.

Gianna opened the drawers of makeup. She put on her foundation and took it a step further by contouring and highlighting before adding her blush. With meticulous precision, she applied a seductive smoky eye shadow that she usually shied away from. A few coats of mascara and then she moved to her brows. Only then did she scrutinize her array of lipsticks.

She looked over her shoulder at the gown that hung waiting for her, then slid her gaze to the chair where her mask still sat in the box.

The color of a woman's lips could either complement an outfit or ruin it. There were many choices, and she couldn't decide. Yet.

So she moved to her hair. After she blew it dry, she ran her hands through the vivid red strands. There would be no bun for her this night. Her hair, like her face, would be changed.

Once she finished, she rose and chose a sexy pair of panties and a strapless bra. Her fingers ran along the edge of the underwear against her stomach.

Then she gazed at the dress. She walked to it and ran her hands over the material. It was a special dress for a special night. Once it was fastened in place and her shoes on, she returned to her vanity. Her hand hovered over the lipsticks as she imagined each shade on her lips. Finally she chose a color.

She didn't look at herself in the mirror as she moved to her dresser and selected a pair of diamond stud earrings and rose gold bracelets that she placed on each wrist.

Next, she reached for her mask and put it on before tying it at the back of her head. With everything in place, she then looked at herself in the mirror.

Now the woman she saw was as changed outside as she was within. She stared at herself, taking it all in and finding that she wasn't just happy about what she glimpsed, but comfortable with it as well.

She walked from her room and down the stairs to grab a shawl and drape it around her shoulders. Then she was out the door and getting onto the boat that would take her to the masquerade ball.

The night was going to be magical. She just knew it.

Chapter Seven

So much for being in control of the situation. Sebastian sighed as he stood with his hands in his pockets and stared out the window, watching the boats moving through the Grand Canal. He'd thought he was in charge of his plan. His skill and expertise were going to make it easy to woo Gianna. Then how the fuck was he the one who'd ended up seduced?

No matter how many times he went over it in his head, he couldn't figure out where things had shifted out of his hands and into hers. What was worse, it didn't appear as if she even knew she had control.

And he couldn't decide if it was better that their kiss had been interrupted—twice, no less—or not. In order to maneuver her where he wanted her, he had to continue with his seduction.

The only problem was that he feared moving forward. Because he no longer wanted to use her as a pawn. Because the thought of causing her hurt made him ill. Because he found her intriguing and irresistible.

The Ice Queen.

Except he wasn't so sure she was made of ice. If she were, wouldn't he be frozen? He was on fire. Scorched, singed, enflamed.

Burned.

Since the moment he'd left her, he'd dug through everything he'd found about her and searched through the list Ryder had given him. He was hoping to find something, some kernel or nugget that would tell him she knew exactly what Mikkel was doing and that she was in on it.

If he knew she was a party to the madness, he could shove aside his attraction and concentrate on helping Ulrik. It wasn't that he was forgetting about his old friend. On the contrary, Sebastian was the only one helping Ulrik.

However, there was no use denying that when he was with Gianna, Sebastian was engrossed with seducing her. What had been his mission was now something he craved desperately.

The knock at the door made him turn his head toward it. His first thought was Gianna, which had him hurrying to it. Whatever hope he'd held vanished when he opened the door and saw the young boy before him holding a box.

"Are you Sebastian?" the boy asked in a thick Italian accent.

"I am."

The boy held out the black box. "This is for you."

Sebastian handed the lad some money and took the box. He held it before him, wondering what it could be as he closed the door. He didn't bother to lock it. There was a barrier around the entire palazzo that kept out Fae and humans alike. The only way they could be allowed in was with his invitation.

Taking the box to the kitchen, he set it on the large island and grasped the lid with both hands. Then he lifted it and peeled back the red tissue paper. Inside was a black leather eye mask. Beneath it was a note with his name scrawled in a neat, sweeping script. He opened the paper and began to read.

Sebastian—

I still don't know why I accepted your proposal today and met you, but you opened my eyes to many things. I would like to thank you for that.

Perhaps you'll accept this mask as well as my invitation to join me at the Masquerade Ball tonight. It starts at eight o'clock at the Byzantine palazzo. I hope to see you there.

Gianna

He set down the note and looked at the mask. Masquerades were a part of the Venetian culture dating back hundreds of years. It was still some time before Carnival began, but he suspected that was why Mikkel was having the ball now.

He closed the box and turned on his heel to make his way into the master chamber and then the closet. In every one of the homes owned by Dreagan, there were clothes and shoes in the style for each of the Kings, as well as their sizes. Including multiple varieties and colors of tuxes.

Sebastian opened a cabinet and found the selection of various masks. Several were voltos, or full-face masks that covered everything but his eyes. A volto would help keep him hidden from Mikkel, but it would prove difficult in his wooing of Gianna. If he went, it could tip his hand that he knew about Mikkel, but it was also a perfect chance to lay eyes on the man and discover if his hunch was right.

Grabbing a half mask, Sebastian laid it on the stool in the middle of the closet and stripped out of his clothes before taking a quick shower. Drying off, he tossed the towel aside and walked naked into the closet, where he chose a modern black tux. He combed his hair back into a queue, and then put on the mask he'd worn five centuries earlier during Carnival.

The Diavolo, or Devil mask, would hide all but his mouth and jaw. It was solid black and made from soft leather. There were two sets of horns at the forehead that gave way to curved temples and sloping cheeks that then came to a point on each side of the mouth. The downward slanted eyes of the mask also helped to hide his identity.

He glanced at the time to see it was just after eight. Sebastian grabbed the black cloak and put it on as he walked out of the palazzo and into the boat that came with the property.

The night felt alive with possibility. His heart thought of Gianna, but his mind only knew one target—Mikkel.

Sebastian was about to start the engine when a form stepped from the dark. He looked into black eyes and set his hands on the steering wheel as he waited.

"You doona look surprised to see me," Constantine said as he stood on the dock.

"Because I'm no'. I knew you'd want to talk to me."

Con nodded and looked around. "I've no' been to Venice in over a thousand years. There is much about the city that hasna changed."

"And much that has."

The King of Kings met his gaze. "You seem verra sure of your theory."

"There are unanswered questions. Someone has to ask them and demand answers."

"And that's you?"

Sebastian thought about it a moment and said, "Aye. It's me because I didna do my part as Ulrik's friend and help him overcome his anger during the war. It's me because I never reached out to him while he was banished. It's me because I know how I feel no' being able to shift, and it's only been a few weeks. He's endured countless centuries. It's me because someone has to stand up for him."

"And I willna?" Con asked, no censor in his words.

"If you were no' King of Kings, I think it would be you here instead of me. I know you can no' follow your heart as we do. You've proved that several times already. Ulrik was your brother, just as he was mine. We three might no' share blood, but our bonds were just as strong."

Con stood there in silence for a long stretch of time. "You're right. Someone does have to ask the questions. I didna tell you that Anson heard the name Mikkel while he was being held by the Dark Fae."

"Why did you no' tell me?" Sebastian asked, not bothering to keep the anger from his words.

"Perhaps because it would be easier to blame only Ulrik."

"Come with me. It should be you here, no' me."

"Once maybe, but no longer. Go find your information, Bast. I hope it's what you believe it to be."

Sebastian felt better knowing that Con was on his side. "If it is?"

"Then we'll deal with it. But be on guard. If this Mikkel is in fact the same dragon we both remember as Ulrik's uncle, he'll be looking for any Dragon King."

"I'll be careful."

"How are you getting in?" Con asked.

Sebastian thought of Gianna, his Ice Queen. "His personal assistant."

"Most likely he keeps tabs on her, which means he could already know of you."

"We might no' get another chance at this bastard."

Con ran his hand over his jaw. "I doona care what you have to do, but doona let Mikkel capture you."

For the first time in hours, Sebastian smiled. "You have my word."

"I expect to hear from you later," Con said as he turned and began to walk away.

Once Con disappeared into the darkness, Sebastian started the engine and backed the boat out of the slip before proceeding the short distance to the Masquerade.

He pulled up to the dock and handed the boat to an attendant before making his way to the carpet-lined dock and stairs. He stood in queue watching as others handed invitations to the guards at the door.

When it came his turn, he looked at the men and said, "I'm the guest of Gianna Santini."

"Your name?" one of them asked without blinking.

"Sebastian," he replied.

Immediately, he was allowed through. The first thing Sebastian noticed was that every decoration for the party was silver with some white, black, and red thrown it. It could be a coincidence, but he doubted it since Ulrik was King of the Silvers.

He moved to the outside of the room and slowly wandered through the crowd. Everyone was decked out in full masquerade costumes, several with the long pointed nose masks. Many of the women had chosen delicate metal masks, while some had full facial masks with huge plumes of feathers sticking up. Only a few men sported the full-face masks.

He was wondering what Mikkel might wear when he looked to the stairs and found his thoughts halted when he caught sight of Gianna. He knew it was her instantly by the flaming hair that fell almost to her waist.

With her hand on the railing, she walked down the stairs her head held high. She wore an eye mask that faded from rose gold to gold and was adorned with gold glitter that looked as if it was made to match her dress.

She looked as regal as a princess in her sleeveless rose gold gown. The bodice had a modest scoop at the front neckline while being covered with pink and champagne colored pearls and sequins that continued down to her hips before fanning out over the full skirt.

When she reached the bottom of the stairs, she turned to talk to someone. Her hair swung out of the way, and Sebastian saw that the dress dipped into a *V* at the small of her back. His hands itched to touch her creamy skin.

She moved about the room as if it was her party, and in many ways it was. He had no doubt that she'd planned every last detail. Every decoration, every *hors d'oeuvre*, and every piece of music being played was all her.

He couldn't take his eyes from her as she spoke with nobles, royalty, and billionaires with a gracious smile, listening intently.

It wasn't until she was making her way toward him that she looked up, their eyes clashing. Her steps slowed as her lips parted before gradually turning up in a smile. She walked past someone trying to talk to her as she came toward him.

Sebastian began walking to her, grabbing two glasses of champagne as he did. They maneuvered around the dancing couples until they met.

Her green eyes searched his. "You came."

"As if I would pass up a chance to see you," he said and handed her a glass.

"It was last minute."

"Sometimes that's when the most fun happens."

Her smile widened as she eyed his mask. "A devil's mask?"

"A family heirloom."

Her smile melted away as she looked at him in wonder. "Who are you?"

She'd asked him that earlier, but he hadn't answered her. Nor would he now. "Does it matter?" he asked.

"No."

"Then dance with me," he said as he took her glass and handed them to a waiter.

Sebastian pulled her into his arms and out onto the dance floor in the next heartbeat.

Chapter Eight

If this were a dream, she would kill whoever woke her. The lights, the music...the man. Gianna wondered if this was what Cinderella felt like at the ball. Not in her wildest dreams did she ever dare to feel this beautiful or think to have a man like Sebastian moving her expertly around the dance floor.

Or for him to look at her as if she was the very center of his world.

She'd known as soon as her gaze clashed with his topaz one that it was Sebastian. His mask might hide his face, but there was no mistaking those gem-like eyes of his. She wasn't upset that he didn't wear her mask. Why would he when he had an antique one?

The Diavolo mask somehow suited him. Not that she thought him a devil, only that there was a lethal combination of confidence and mystery about him that had drawn her in from the very beginning.

And if she thought he looked good before, he was mouth-watering, devastatingly gorgeous in his tailored tux. Though she had to admit to wanting to unbind his hair and run her fingers through it.

Without a doubt, he was the most handsome man at the ball. She didn't stop and wonder why he was with her, she simply enjoyed every second of it.

How the slow, sensual music filled the room. How everyone ceased to exist. How he stared intently into her eyes. How he moved her. How his fingers pressed against her bare back. How he pulled her against him so their bodies were molded to each other.

"In all my life, I've never seen anything so beautiful," he said with his husky brogue.

By the intensity of his gaze, the words weren't merely a compliment, but something he truly believed. Chills raced over her.

"Since I've first seen you I've wanted to take your hair down to see how long it was. It's likes strands of fire flowing down your back to tease my hand with its touch."

His words made it impossible to breathe. Her breath rushed past her lips as her chest heaved and her lungs fought to pull in more air. But it was a useless battle as long as she was in Sebastian's arms.

His lips turned up slightly at the corners as his eyes fairly burned with a light from within. "I can feel the energy, the inferno within you. You burn with it," he finished with a rough whisper.

Her heart tripped over itself. An inferno? Yes. She felt it. It was blazing inside—all because of him.

"My Ice Queen," he murmured. "Let the fire consume you."

Didn't he know it already was? Couldn't he tell?

His smile widened and she saw his eyes crinkle. "Aye."

He maneuvered them off the floor and through the crowd onto the balcony. The night air brushed against her skin, but it didn't cool her. Because being alone with Sebastian only made her passion flare higher.

The music wafted through the open doors as he brought her against him once more. This time his splayed hand moved up her back until he was cupping her head. She didn't tell herself to be cautious, that this couldn't be real. None of that was significant when she felt this good. No matter what tomorrow brought, she was going to live tonight. Even if she did fly too close to the sun in the process.

The fall back to earth was going to be worth it.

"Gianna," he whispered before he lowered his head.

Her eyes drifted shut as she waited for the kiss. His lips were soft, firm as he pressed them against hers. The first brush of his mouth was gentle. The second more insistent. By the third, her lips parted at the feel of his tongue.

She slid her arms around his neck and leaned to the side when he deepened the kiss. Within seconds, she was clutching him as their passion exploded and the kiss grew frenzied, feverish.

His thumb caressed across her jaw as he slowly ended the kiss. "I want you," he said when he lifted his head. "That isna true. I *need* you."

Oh God. She might faint. She was dizzy from the passion that thrummed through her, blistering her with its strength. And then for him to say something like that.

"I've wanted to kiss you all day, and now that I have, I want more," he continued.

She licked her lips, feeling them tingle from his kisses. "So do I."

"Ach, lass. Doona say such things to me now. I burn too hot for you."

Gianna knew exactly how he felt. His words and that amazing voice of his were only making things worse. "I don't want what I'm feeling to stop."

"You deserve better than me lifting your skirts and taking you right here."

Heat flooded her sex at the thought.

Sebastian mumbled something incoherent beneath his breath and moved her to the side of the balcony into the shadows. He claimed her mouth in a savage kiss that only spurred her desires higher.

To her shock—and delight—his hand cupped her knee through the layers of her gown and lifted, setting her foot on the edge of a bench. Her stomach fluttered with anticipation when that same hand found her ankle and slowly skimmed up the outside of her leg beneath her skirts.

When he reached her hip, he ended the kiss and said her name. She peeled open her eyes and was caught in his gaze. He refused to let her look away as his hand caressed across her leg to the inside of her thigh.

She dug her fingers in his neck when his hand brushed against her sex. Her body froze, anticipation making her heart thump against her ribs. It was his thumb that ran along the crotch of her panties, teasing her aching flesh.

"You're wet," he murmured.

All thought ceased when his fingers moved against her more firmly. Then he hooked a digit at the seam of her panties and moved them to the side. She was panting as she impatiently waited for him to touch her. He prolonged her agony by caressing against the juncture of her leg and then playing with her trimmed curls.

Finally, she felt his fingers on her, moving over her woman's lips before sliding inside her. Almost immediately he pulled his fingers out. She whimpered, needing to feel him deep.

But that whimper turned into a gasp when his thumb circled her clit leisurely, gradually increasing his pace. She rocked her hips against him, seeking the release her body craved. She saw his enjoyment in the way his eyes flashed before darkening with desire.

If she thought he would end things quickly, she soon discovered how wrong she was. Sebastian teased her mercilessly. While he played with her clit, he would thrust his fingers inside her every so often.

He brought her to the edge of orgasm effortlessly, only to move his hand away as he kissed her. She lost count of how many times he brought her to the brink.

"Do you feel your fire?" he whispered against her ear.

Gianna nodded. "Yes."

His groan made her rock her hips faster. She had never done anything so carnal, so erotic. She'd never felt so...sexual. As if every cell, every nerve only wanted one thing—pleasure.

"Look at me," he demanded."

She opened her eyes and gasped at the desire that had tightened his face. She wasn't the only one burning for release.

"I'm no' done with you," he stated. "This is merely the beginning. Do you understand?"

"I understand."

As soon as the words passed her lips, he began moving his fingers within her, stroking her higher and higher. When she didn't think she could take any more, he began to thumb her clit.

His mouth covered hers, silencing her cry as pleasure erupted within her, filling her with such ecstasy that it took her breath away. The bliss swept her away while seizing her body, until all she could do was give in to all of it.

With her sex still pulsing, he moved her panties back into place and lowered her leg. Then he held her, his arms wrapped tightly around her until she could breathe normally again. Gianna didn't want to return to the ball. She'd much rather go somewhere to be alone with Sebastian so she could explore his body as he'd begun to do with hers.

The change in the music let her know that Oscar had arrived and was about to make an entrance. She straightened from Sebastian and looked up at him.

"Work?" he asked.

She blew out a breath. "Unfortunately. Will you stay?"

"You'll know when I leave, because you'll be with me."

A thrill shot through her. She smiled in response, her heart missing a beat.

"Go," he urged. "Do what you need."

She reluctantly stepped out of his arms. Before moving through the open doors and back into the palazzo, she shook out her skirts to make sure everything was in place. Then, with her head high, she walked toward the stairs, where everyone was looking.

Her employer wore a silver half-mask with some engravings that began along the side of his right eye before dipping under it and across the nose and moving over the left eye, stopping beside it.

His long hair was down, loose about his shoulders. Not once had she ever known him to color the gray at his temples, despite him looking much too young to have any. He was physically fit and amazingly handsome, though she'd never been attracted to him. Which was odd, since every other woman seemed to be.

Much like they were with Sebastian.

She smiled as she thought about their interlude. Though she had been well pleasured, she wanted more. She yearned to feel Sebastian deep inside her. Putting him and their passion aside, she smiled at Oscar as he raised a glass of champagne at the top of the stairs. She didn't pay attention as he toasted the people and the party.

Gianna glanced over her shoulder to find Sebastian in the doorway of the balcony, his gaze fastened on Oscar. She returned her attention to her employer as he made his way down the stairs to her.

"As I promised, everything is in order," she told him.

His gold eyes gazed over her shoulder. She turned, thinking about Sebastian, but he was no longer there. Disappointed, she looked at Oscar. "Sir?"

"You look different."

Unable to help it, she blushed. "I love a masquerade," she explained.

"I was told you were seen dancing. You never dance."

His sudden interest in her private life made her uncomfortable. "Of course I've danced before."

"Who was the man dancing with you tonight?"

She smiled, having no intention of revealing that information because it was none of his business. Which was odd. Gianna would've never held back before but that was another part of her that changed. "You have others waiting to speak with you, so I won't hold you up any longer."

She motioned to the band to begin playing as she walked away. The hairs on the back of her neck were standing on end, and she had the distinct impression that Oscar was staring at her. As much as she wanted to, she refused to turn and check.

After making a few stops to talk, she looked up and found Sebastian. He smiled at her, and though she wished to be with him, she knew Oscar was watching.

She made her way to Sebastian, suddenly uneasy about him being there. As if she was a teenager and had been caught in a lie with her parent. Which was silly. She was a grown woman who answered to no one.

"What is it?" he asked when she reached him.

"My employer was asking about you."

Was it her imagination or had Sebastian tensed? His gaze was locked on Oscar. "Did he indeed?"

"It made me uncomfortable in a way I can't explain."

He looked down at her then. "You wish for me to keep my distance?"

"If you don't mind. I'm very private about my life, and—"

"You doona need to explain more. I understand. I'll be around. When you're ready to leave, I'll be waiting."

She watched as he turned to walk away, only to come to a halt as if kicked. Gianna looked to where his gaze had landed and found a guest who was among half of the men in complete masquerade costume, which included a cloak that covered his head, a full-face mask, and a tricorn hat.

Sebastian and the stranger stared at each other for a long minute. Then a group moved between them, and once they passed, the man was gone. Unable to help herself, she began looking for the stranger. Maybe it was because of Sebastian's reaction, but she had a feeling the stranger was important.

Chapter Nine

Ulrik. Sebastian knew it the moment his gaze locked with the golden ones. He saw through the Volto mask of all white with the intricate silver that framed the eyes, nose, and forehead before moving down the cheeks. That same silver covered the lips on the mask.

Every inch of Ulrik was covered, but there was no mistaking those eyes—the same eyes Sebastian had seen on Mikkel, who also happened to be Gianna's employer.

What Sebastian didn't know was why Ulrik was there. Was he working with Mikkel? Or against him?

There was so much Sebastian wanted to say to Ulrik, to let him know. But the twenty feet separating them felt as wide as the ocean. Had too much time passed? Was Ulrik beyond redemption? Was he so far gone that the only way to give him peace was in death?

Of all the Dragon Kings, Sebastian had always thought Ulrik would be the one to survive them all. Mainly because Ulrik had loved and accepted everyone. He saw the world as something bright and beautiful, a place to live each day to the fullest. It was rare for Ulrik's anger to last longer than a few minutes. He knew the benefit of forgiveness and compassion, of tolerance and mercy.

It was what made Ulrik see joy and love in all things from dragons to mortals to animals to plants. More times than not, when anyone came upon Ulrik, he was laughing. His happiness was infectious to all who came in contact with him.

What even fewer knew was that Con had been just like Ulrik in his youth.

The bond that had always held fast between Con and Ulrik splintered when Con bound Ulrik's magic and sent him away. Sebastian spent more time sleeping in his mountain than awake. Perhaps that was the reason he didn't hold such resentment toward Ulrik as the rest of the Kings did.

But the reason didn't signify. Ulrik mattered. Con mattered.

Their friendship mattered.

Sebastian lifted his foot to close the distance between him and Ulrik when a group came between them. He tried to keep his eye on Ulrik, but in the space of half a second, his friend was gone.

Disappointment filled Sebastian as he closed his eyes for a moment. There would be another chance. There had to be. Ulrik would know that he hadn't been abandoned by at least one of his brothers.

Sebastian opened his eyes and continued to the back of the room. He wasn't at all happy to see Gianna visibly shaken by Mikkel's intrusive questions. But it had been expected. He'd hoped to stay out of Mikkel's way in order to observe him, but it had only been a matter of time before Mikkel discovered a Dragon King was in attendance.

Perhaps the fact Mikkel didn't have that knowledge was why he was asking Gianna such questions. No doubt if Mikkel knew a King was here, the night would be going much differently.

It was easy for Sebastian to move about the ball with his mask, though he spotted some men who were searching for a guest. Most likely for him. Not that he was worried about being found. It was going to take more than some men following Gianna and seeing who she spoke with to find him.

Though he remained close to Mikkel, Sebastian kept his eye on Gianna as well. While he searched the crowd several times, he never saw Ulrik again. But the proof he needed stood before him—if only Mikkel would take off his mask.

Sebastian made his way up the stairs to look down upon the party. The next few hours crawled by, leaving him thinking of Gianna more and more. He hadn't intended to do more than kiss her on the balcony, but the look she gave him had smashed whatever control he had.

The feel of her in his arms as desire made her green eyes glow had pushed him past the point of reason. It was her moans and soft cries of pleasure that'd had him teetering on the edge himself. It was only the noise of the passing boats and the party within that stopped him from taking her right then.

But he'd known from the moment he saw her that his Ice Queen was a sleeping volcano waiting to explode.

"She's verra beautiful."

His head jerked sideways at the sound of the voice behind him. A voice he hadn't heard in ages. "Ulrik."

"Doona turn around."

Sebastian swung his gaze to the right and down to where Mikkel stood with four other men. "What are you doing here?"

"I could ask you the same question," Ulrik said.

"I'm here because—"

But Ulrik spoke over him. "You shouldna have come. You've put the woman's life in danger."

"Are you threatening her?" Sebastian tensed. He didn't want to fight Ulrik, but he would.

It took him a moment to realize that he was willing to fight a friend over the idea of Gianna being hurt. As confusing as that was, he shoved it aside to mull over later.

"If I was, I wouldna warn you," Ulrik replied tersely.

Sebastian drew in a deep breath and released it. "I willna allow her to be harmed."

"Then you should've thought twice about involving her in whatever you're up to. Leave Venice. Before it's too late, Bast."

He spun around when Ulrik said his name, but once again he'd disappeared. Sebastian slowly turned back and scanned the crowd for Gianna. There were three men following her. Two were obvious, but there was a third that Sebastian almost overlooked because he was so good.

Ulrik's words repeated in his head like a drum. Sebastian was responsible for the men following Gianna. He was to blame for Mikkel's sudden interest in her private life. And if Sebastian didn't do something, he might very well be liable for her death also.

Gianna had begun as nothing more than an objective to woo in order to obtain the much-needed information about Mikkel. Sebastian had intended to do whatever it took to win her over, and he would've left her without a second thought.

That was then. Now...now he comprehended with crystal clarity just what he'd dragged her into. If she was innocent of knowing who Mikkel really was, then his actions were even more reprehensible.

But he couldn't just leave, as Ulrik suggested, either. Now that Mikkel's attention was on her, there was no telling what the bastard would do.

The more Sebastian watched Mikkel, the more he saw the arse look Gianna's way every few minutes, as if keeping tabs on her. As if it wasn't enough that the men were following her.

Sebastian saw Gianna turn her head this way and that casually. She was looking for him. Right before she lifted her gaze to the second floor, he took several steps back. Whether he liked it or not, Gianna couldn't be seen with him again that night. That also meant that she couldn't leave with him as they'd planned.

"*Scusami*, excuse me," said a voice behind him.

Sebastian sighed. He'd really hoped to avoid such an interaction, but it looked as though his luck had run out. He turned around to look at the man in a silver and black eye mask who spoke.

"*Signore?*" the man asked.

Sebastian remained silent.

"Will you come with me?" he asked in broken English.

Since there were a few people watching him, Sebastian followed the guard toward a door. As soon as they were through it, he noted a narrow stairway down. Sebastian then grabbed the guard and slammed his head against the stone hard enough to knock him out.

He hefted the man over his shoulder and carried him down the rest of the stairs. There were two doors. He used his enhanced hearing to determine that the door to the right had no one behind it. He quietly opened it and slipped inside.

The room was small and used for storage. He bent and sat the man up. A quick search produced rope and tape. He covered the man's mouth before binding his hands and feet. Then Sebastian slipped back out the entry and up the stairs.

Instead of returning through the door he'd left, he kept climbing the stairs to the next floor. When he came to the landing, he walked to the door and put his hand on the knob, slowly turning. It made a loud squeak, but thankfully it was drowned out by the music from below.

Sebastian opened the door and walked through it before closing it behind him. He looked to either side of him in the corridor to find multiple doors. By the sounds of approaching footsteps, precautions had been made to prevent guests from venturing upstairs.

He saw a door cracked open and peeked inside. The moment his gaze landed on a Dark Fae, he had confirmation Mikkel was the culprit. While Ulrik was the type of tactician who would use anything and everything at his disposal, the masquerade wasn't a battle. The Ulrik he knew wouldn't bring the Fae to such an event.

All Sebastian needed was a photo of Mikkel as evidence, something he couldn't get at the ball with everyone wearing masks.

Now wasn't the time to confront the Dark. There were too many mortals about who would only get in the way and most likely killed. His need to kill the Dark would have to wait for another day.

He turned and retraced his steps. It was time he disappeared.

* * * *

Mikkel ended his conversation with a prince and walked to Gianna. He couldn't shake the feeling that something was amiss. He couldn't put his finger on it, but everything pointed to his assistant.

It all began when she took the morning off. That was something she never did, especially when there was an event that day. Her dancing was a rare thing indeed, but it was something she'd done before.

It was the way she dressed, as if she wanted to look sexy. In all the years she'd worked for him, not once had he seen her hair down. Then there was her makeup and the way she carried herself. That was something a woman did when she wanted to gain someone's attention.

However, the most telling aspect of it all was the smile she'd worn all night. He knew the look of a woman who had been well pleasured, and Gianna wore that expression with ease. The question was—who had she taken to her bed?

There was a niggling worry that the Dragon Kings might discover him before he was ready to expose his plans, but he'd taken such precautions that he was sure it was just paranoia.

Unless it wasn't.

It could be Ulrik. It would be just like his nephew to create such a stir. But Ulrik's time was limited. Already the Druid had him in her sights. Soon, Ulrik wouldn't be meddling in anything.

The more Mikkel thought about it, the more he knew it had to be Ulrik who was paying Gianna attention. And he knew just how to catch his nephew.

Gianna gasped and jerked her head to him when Mikkel grabbed her arm right above the elbow. Her anger disappeared as soon as she saw him. "Sir? Is everything all right?"

He pulled her away from the group she was talking to with an apology and moved her to the edge of the dance floor. "I'm sorry to have doubted you about the ball. Nothing is out of place."

"I've never let you down before."

Her tight smile didn't bother him as he kept his hold on her. "I was told you invited someone for yourself. I'd very much like to meet him."

"Of course," she hurriedly said. "Did I overstep by inviting him?"

"Not at all. After all the fine work you've done for me and the fact you never ask for such things for yourself, I don't see the harm in it. This once."

Behind her mask, her gaze darted away. Mikkel's disappointment in Gianna was great. She was one of the few he didn't have to remind of their places in this world.

Until now. Until Ulrik.

"Take me to him," Mikkel ordered.

She looked around, shaking her head. "I...I don't see him."

"Let's take a walk around then. Perhaps we'll find him."

He kept Gianna by his side as he waved at his guests and ignored those who called him over to talk. After walking the entire expanse of the party, including the balconies, they had yet to find Ulrik.

Gianna forcefully pulled her arm from his grasp. She raised her chin and said, "Excuse me. There are things I need to see to if you want to keep the party running smoothly."

He stared after her. She was a good employee, but the moment he suspected disloyalty he took action. It was too bad she was going to have to die.

Chapter Ten

Gianna didn't think there had ever been another time in her life where she'd been so happy one second and so miserable the next.

The masquerade was meant to be her night. It had begun with excitement that only intensified with Sebastian's arrival. Being in his arms as he moved them around the floor while they danced had been the stuff of her dreams as a little girl.

Their time on the balcony with their feverish kisses and the way he had brought her to orgasm with his fingers had been her fantasy as a woman.

The night couldn't have been going better or more magically. Then Oscar made his appearance and everything had fallen apart, as if midnight had come and her fairy godmother had taken everything away.

Gianna stood on the balcony with her arms wrapped around herself and sighed as the clock struck four. The last of the guests had finally departed and the cleanup had begun. Normally she would be on her way home, but she remained, hoping for some sign of Sebastian.

Had one of Oscar's guards found him? Had Oscar spoken to him? Those were the only explanations she could come up with that Sebastian would leave after assuring her that he'd wait.

Oscar's bizarre behavior once he learned she had invited a guest, and then his perplexing interest in Sebastian, disturbed her. So many times that evening she'd felt Oscar's gaze on her, making her apprehensive.

She'd been thankful that Sebastian kept his distance because of it, but now she wished that she had kept him by her side. Why should she be embarrassed for having a good time? Why should she have to apologize for having a life?

Sure, she'd overstepped by giving Sebastian an invitation without approval, but that wasn't a big deal. Sebastian obviously came from money and breeding, so it wasn't as if he didn't know how to act in such circumstances. In fact, she wasn't sure she'd seen Sebastian talk to anyone.

The only one who seemed to get his attention was that man in the white and silver mask. The way Sebastian had stared at the man was like they knew each other. She didn't understand it since she could barely make out the man's eyes through the mask, much less his hair color because of the hood on the cloak and then the hat.

When she saw the crew begin to roll up the carpet from the dock, she knew it was time to go. Oscar had departed hours ago. She wasn't sure why he had the palazzo, since he rarely stayed within its walls.

She dropped her arms and turned to walk into the house. As soon as she was inside, servants hurried to close the balcony doors and lock them. It was sad that such a grand house would be closed up again, forgotten until there was a need for another party. It was why she came and walked the halls every few months.

Gianna made her way toward the front hall where a guard held her wrap. She didn't say a word as she grabbed the shawl and strode out the front door to the dock. She waited fifteen minutes before she realized that all the boats were gone, all the while thinking about how Sebastian had promised they would leave together. But he was nowhere in sight.

With a sigh, she returned to the palazzo and walked out the back entrance to the street. It was only a few blocks until she could find another place to get a boat home. Her heels clicked loudly on the pavement. The night was eerily quiet for Venice. Perhaps it was because she was used to the noise from the party, but she was sensitive to the silence that caused chills to race up her spine.

The shawl did little to help keep her warm. If only she hadn't remained so long on the balcony she could've found a boat and now she'd be sitting in a nice hot bath—or curled beneath her covers.

Her steps slowed when the street narrowed. There were dozens of shadows where anyone could be lurking about, waiting to harm her. She looked behind her to spot a cat racing across the street to disappear in the darkness.

She took a deep breath as she faced forward. Then she started walking. She passed the first shadow, then the second, and a third without anything happening. It was as she neared the fourth that hands reached out and grabbed her. She fought against the hold even as a hand clamped over her mouth to stop her screams.

"Gianna. It's me."

It took a second for the voice to register. When it did, she stilled. Sebastian! As soon as his hand dropped away, she spun out of his arms and glared at him. He was still in his tux and cloak, but the mask was gone.

He held up his hands, palms out, before him. "Easy, lass."

"Easy?" she repeated in dismay. "You just scared ten years off my life."

His lips flattened in a look of regret as he lowered his arms. "That wasna my intent, but I didna know if those men were still following you."

"I don't know why Oscar had those two men trailing me."

"Three," Sebastian corrected her.

She frowned, a growing sense of dread filling her. "Three?"

"You were too occupied with the others to notice him."

"Obviously." And she didn't like the feeling that provoked within her.

He held out his hand to her. "I didna mean to frighten you."

"You said you'd wait for me."

"So I did. Just no' inside the palazzo. I didna like the...interest the guards suddenly took in me."

She winced and lowered her gaze to the ground in embarrassment. "I'm sorry." She looked back up at him. "I don't know what was wrong with Oscar tonight."

"Just so you know, I made sure you had no choice but to walk this path tonight. I was watching to make sure no one harmed you. But I had to see you." He took a step closer, their bodies brushing. "After the passion on the balcony, I need another kiss."

"Just a kiss?"

His lips twisted in a sensual smile. "I want much more than that."

She watched his fingers entangle with hers before caressing up her arm. She tilted her head to the side and raised her gaze to him. "Just what is it you want?"

"You," he replied in a deep timbre. "Naked. On my bed. And writhing in need."

As he spoke, she saw all of it in her mind. Her breathing hitched as her sex clenched. "And?"

"I'm going to spread those long legs of yours and taste what my fingers felt this night."

Her knees threatened to buckle at the wicked promise of his words.

His arm snaked around her, yanking her against his hard chest. He leaned down until his lips brushed her ear. "I'm going to fill you. Then I'll make you come again so I can feel your walls tightening around me."

"What are you waiting for?" she asked breathlessly.

Without another word, he took her hand and started walking. She had to almost run to keep up with him, and despite the need pounding through her, she noticed how he kept them to the shadows at all times.

Finally, they reached the palazzo. She wanted to admire it, but no sooner were they in the door than his mouth was on hers. She let the shawl drop to the floor as he walked her backward.

She shoved his jacket over his shoulders and down his arms, where it landed on the floor. As they continued their journey, her mask was the next thing removed.

Their passion was interrupted by a brief moment of laughter when he couldn't get his shoe off. Sebastian had to bend down and remove it, then she was back in his arms and being kissed as if there was no tomorrow.

She managed to remove her heels right before they reached the stairs. He held up her skirts so she wouldn't trip as she resumed her backward trek. She used that time to grab his shirt and yanked it open, causing buttons to pop off.

His answering groan made her heart race in excitement.

There was a loud ripping noise as Sebastian yanked the shirt from his arms and threw it on the stairs. By the time they reached the top, he had unzipped her gown. After she let it fall from her arms, he lifted her out of it as she stepped over the dress. She reached for the waist of his pants as soon as her feet were back on the ground.

Her fingers fumbled with the zipper before finally opening it and shoving the pants down his hips. He kicked out of the trousers as they reached a doorway and he maneuvered her inside.

Only then did he break the kiss. He gazed at her a long time, and she took the same opportunity with the moonlight flooding through the windows. Then she reached up and loosened the strap on his hair before running her fingers through the thick strands.

Her breath came out in a rush when she realized he was already naked. She flattened her hands over his chest and was awed at the corded muscles. She'd sensed, and even felt his power, but she hadn't expected this.

She smoothed her hands over his wide, thick shoulders and bulging arms. Returning to his chest, she caressed down his stomach to his rock-hard abdomen that narrowed to a trim waist.

Her eyes moved lower to the arousal that stood straining between them, a drop of pre-cum already formed on the head.

"You've had me in this state since I lifted your skirts earlier," he said.

She could look at his body all day. Even his legs... Her thoughts came to a halt when she saw the tattoo. She'd been so intent on his muscles that she'd somehow missed the dragon head on his right side that came over onto his abdomen.

Her fingers ran over the open jaws of the dragon that had fire coming from his mouth in a curious mix of black and red ink. She traced the tattoo of the flames to his navel. But that was only a part of the tat. She spread her palm at the head of the dragon once more and leaned to the side to find that it wrapped around him. Unable to resist, she walked around Sebastian, following the tat partially over his right ass cheek before moving down his leg.

To her shock, the body of the dragon—including its tucked wings—wrapped around and around his leg. She returned to stand in front of Sebastian to follow the tail that ended atop his foot.

There was something different about this tattoo. She didn't know what it was and couldn't place her finger on it, but she was sure of it.

Then she saw her right foot beside his. Atop her foot was the dragon tat she had regretted getting for years. Odd how she no longer felt that way. Then again, there were a lot of unusual things happening since Sebastian walked into her life.

She slowly lifted her gaze until she met his. "Do you believe in Fate?"

"I didna. No' until I saw your tat."

Was it just coincidence that she had a dragon tat? Granted,

Sebastian's tattoo was much different than hers, but there was a connection there. She could feel it.

It was a tangible thing.

"Are you frightened?" he asked.

"Yes."

A small frown formed on his forehead. "Do you want to leave?"

"No."

His fingers grasped her hair, which had fallen over her shoulder. He wound it around his finger, and then his fist. "My Ice Queen is following the fire."

She kept her gaze locked with his as she unhooked her bra. It fell to the floor unheeded. When his eyes sparked with desire, she reached for him, needing the contact of their bodies.

"Come walk in the fire with me," he bade as his other hand slid around her waist.

That's when she surrendered herself to him. She knew then that she would follow Sebastian anywhere.

He was fire.

She was ice.

But with him... She burned.

Chapter Eleven

Desire raged. Passion flared.

The only thing he craved, the only thing he hungered for, was the mortal in his arms. Sebastian moaned as their tongues tangled, enflaming their need.

From the moment he'd brought her to climax on the balcony, he'd been past the point of no return. He recognized that now, accepted it.

Welcomed it.

There was nothing that could tear him out of her arms. A force had bound them, and he had no interest in severing it—even though he realized that every second he spent with her only tightened their bonds.

He continued to kiss her in the moonlight, holding her hair in one hand and her in the other. Her inspection of his dragon tat had touched something deep within him.

"I need you," she whispered between kisses.

Sebastian backed her to the bed with measured steps. Once they reached it, he pushed her backward, following her down onto the mattress.

He rose up on his hands as he ended the kiss to look down at her. Slowly he unwound her hair from his fist and spread it around her. Her green eyes watched him while her hands roamed over his chest and back.

When he released the last fiery lock, he let his gaze run over her amazing body. His hand followed his eyes from the slim column of her throat over her collarbones and between her breasts.

He paused and leisurely cupped a breast before bending to take a turgid nipple into his mouth and swirl his tongue around it. He moved to her other breast and repeated his teasing.

The sound of her quick intake of breath made his balls tighten. Though he longed to continue playing with her sensitive breasts, he continued his exploration down to her stomach.

He circled her navel twice, her responding grin making everything worthwhile. His hand caressed from one hip to the other as he rolled to the side to better see her.

As soon as he glimpsed the patch of red curls, he moaned. Then he slid his fingers down her stomach to the triangle of hair that covered her. As soon as his hand was there, she rocked her hips.

He glanced up to find lips parted as her breath came in gasps. Her half-closed eyes watched, silently begging him to move his fingers lower. To delve into her wet heat as he had done on the balcony.

But he had something else in mind.

Sebastian rose from the bed while he stroked down the outside of her limbs to her feet before smoothing his palms upward along the inside of her legs.

Her eyes were closed now, her fingers fisting the comforter. He watched her as he knelt before the bed and pushed his hands out, spreading her legs—just as he'd told her he would. His mouth hovered over her sex as he blew softly. She whimpered, her fingers tightening in the covers. There was nothing frigid or frozen about his Ice Queen now. She was liquid fire—inside and out.

He blew again, focusing on her swollen clit. She began panting, her body tensing. He rubbed his hands along her inner thighs, allowing his thumbs to brush against her sex.

Only then did he put his mouth on her. She jerked at the contact, a cry falling from her lips. He kept his gaze on her face as he began to flick his tongue over her clit. Her back arched off the bed as a moan filled the room.

To see—and feel—her letting go of all her restraints, surrendering to the passion that shrouded them, made something within him shift. It was subtle, but profound.

He savored the taste of her desire. The louder her cries, the more he continued his assault. He swirled his tongue around her clit until her head was thrashing back and forth. When her body tensed, alerting him that she was close to peaking, he rose up and over her.

When she arched her back, his lips were waiting to wrap around her nipple. As he suckled at her breast, his fingers delved deep inside her, thrusting in time with his tongue.

He massaged her small, pert breast with his free hand as he moved from one nipple to the other. Her arousal and cries of pleasure were only pushing him to bring her to greater heights. He wanted to shatter the ice around her so that she would only know fire—his fire.

His dragon fire.

He groaned at the thought of her standing within his fire. He knew it wasn't possible. Dragon fire was the hottest thing on the planet. Nothing and no one could survive dragon fire other than a Dragon King.

But the fantasy was already implanted in his mind.

"Please," Gianna begged hoarsely.

He lifted his head to kiss along her neck as his fingers continued to thrust inside her. "What is it you want?"

"I need to... I can't take any more."

He smiled against her skin and licked her neck before increasing the tempo of his hand. "What do you need? Tell me."

"I need to come. So...close. P-please."

Sebastian nipped at her earlobe and whispered, "As you wish."

He shifted his thumb to rub against her clit as his fingers plunged inside her. This time when her climax took her, he didn't cover her mouth. He watched the sweet release cross her face as pleasure consumed her.

Her walls clutched around his fingers for a second time that night. No longer could he wait to be inside her. With her body still shuddering from her orgasm, he moved her farther up on the bed.

Her lids lifted and green eyes met his. She pulled him over her and between her legs. Then she reached between them and wrapped her fingers around his cock. He groaned at the feel of her stroking up and down his length. His hips began to rock forward, the hunger for her clawing at him.

With their gazes locked, she took the head of his arousal and brought it to her entrance. He clenched his jaw at the feel of her wetness. He couldn't remember the last time he'd craved a woman so. The more he thought of it, the more he began to suspect he hadn't truly felt this kind of passion before.

He pushed his hips forward, sliding inside her slick walls gradually so she could take all of him. When she had taken every last inch of him, she lifted her legs and wrapped them around his waist.

She was wonderfully tight and hot. It was everything Sebastian could do to hold onto the last shreds of his control. He wanted to claim Gianna, to mark her so that everyone knew she was his Ice Queen.

Her nails lightly scraped up his spine to his neck before her fingers threaded in his hair. She placed the palm of her other hand on his side and urged him forward.

He began rocking his hips, his cock sliding in and out of her in a slow, steady rhythm with short strokes. With every shift of his hips, of entering her, of filling her, he could almost feel the links connecting them tighten, strengthen.

Tomorrow would bring a new set of problems, ones he refused to think about right now. Not when he had a woman like Gianna in his arms and his bed.

"More," she demanded.

He smiled at his greedy lover and gave her what she wanted. His hips pumped faster. Pleasure crossed her face as her eyes rolled back in her head.

She lifted her hips to match him, sending them spiraling down an abyss of desire. Their harsh breaths filled the room as their bodies rocked against each other, slick with sweat. He drove inside her deep as her cries grew louder. As he felt himself drawing closer to his own climax, he didn't stop it. Not that he could have even if he'd wanted to.

Gianna had seeped into his soul, his very being. He was attuned to her in a way that he'd never been with another individual. He could feel her heart beat, sense her breath as it left her.

With long, hard thrusts, he stroked her body into a fever pitch that matched his own. They were on a precipice, clinging to each other right before they fell.

It was the walls of her sex clutching around his cock and her shout of desire as she climaxed that sent him tipping over the edge. He gave one last thrust and felt his seed fill her. For that moment, it was more than their bodies that connected.

When their breathing calmed, he rolled onto his side and brought her against his body. In the aftermath of their frenzied lovemaking, they simply held each other.

An untold number of minutes passed before Gianna drew in a breath and said, "My ex-husband wasn't cruel. He never beat me or cheated on me. He simply refused to see me."

Sebastian couldn't fathom her words. How could anyone not see the beautiful, fiery woman that she was?

"I shouldn't have married him, but he let me do whatever I wanted while we dated. I knew he would never stop me from pursuing whatever I wished. And I was right. He didn't. Because he didn't care. When I finally came to that conclusion, I filed for divorce. I thought he would be as indifferent about it as our marriage, but he wasn't. He contested it."

Sebastian tightened his arm around her as he felt the pain of her words.

"He fought me on everything, and it just grew too painful. I gave in to whatever he wanted just to get out of the marriage. He's one of the reasons I fled New York. I wanted to put the past behind me," she said.

He kissed her forehead. "I think that was wise. Do you still have contact with him?"

"I changed all my numbers so he couldn't find me. Have you ever been married?" She looked up at him and wrinkled her nose. "I probably should've asked if you were married before I let things go this far."

Sebastian shook his head. "I'm no' now, nor ever have been married."

"Afraid of commitment?"

"In a manner."

"That's either a yes or a no."

He glanced at the dark beamed ceiling and put one arm behind his head. "I'm no' afraid of giving myself to the right person."

"I find it hard to fathom that a man who looks as good as you is alone."

"But I am."

She rested her head on his chest as her arm draped across him. "I can't stop thinking of Oscar and his interest in you. It's just so odd."

"Have you brought many men around him?"

"No," she said hesitantly. "But he's never cared about my private life before." She raised her head and looked at him again, resting her chin on his chest. "Why do I think this has to do with you?"

Sebastian smoothed a lock of hair out of her face and behind her ear. "I believe your employer might be a connection to helping me find Ulrik."

For long moments, she stared at him. He could see her piecing it all together. He wasn't sure if she was going to explode in anger or become frozen with outrage.

She surprised him by merely saying, "You sought me out."

"I could lie, but I willna."

"So you used me." She sat up and looked around the room before focusing on his face once more. "Yet you never asked me anything about Oscar. Not once."

He shook his head, studying her. "Nay."

She nodded as she snorted in derision. "You wanted to go to the party and you didn't even have to ask me. I gave you the invitation."

"The party allowed me to see him, which I needed to do." He pulled his arm from behind his head and licked his lips. "I'm sorry."

"What's the connection between Oscar and Ulrik?" she demanded.

Chapter Twelve

Gianna waited for Sebastian's answer. She was hurt to realize that she'd been used, but she couldn't say she was sorry. What he had given her was worth his deception.

Going forward, however, was going to be another matter.

"I believe Oscar is doing things and putting the blame on Ulrik," Sebastian said.

She frowned at his words. "What do you mean? What things?"

"Killings."

Sadly, she wasn't as surprised as she probably should've been. Perhaps it was because Oscar was so secretive that she could imagine such events going on.

She blew out a breath. "Is Ulrik being charged with these murders?"

"No' exactly."

"You're being vague. I don't like that." She turned to crawl out of the bed when Sebastian's arm looped around her and dragged her back.

"Wait," he murmured against her ear from behind. "Let me explain."

She contemplated his proposal for a minute before nodding her head. Since their first encounter she'd been drawn to him. Even if she should leave, she couldn't. There was no other choice for her but to agree. As soon as she did, he released her. She turned to face him, catching sight of the dragon tattoo on his abdomen again.

"I have to be ambiguous. There are things you shouldna be a part of," he said.

She rolled her eyes in frustration. "What is it? Drugs? The mob?

Guns?"

"What?" he asked in confusion. Then he gave a firm shake of his head. "Nay, none of that."

"Then what is it that I can't know?"

"Gianna, please," he said. "Already you've brought Oscar's attention to you. Leave things alone."

She raised her brows. "How, when you want information from me?"

"No' anymore," Sebastian said and slowly lay back.

His words should've appeased her. Instead, she grew agitated. "Too bad. I'm already involved."

"I was wrong to bring you into this. I'll find another way."

She shook her head. "If there had been another way, you would've taken it. You had to have a plan in case I didn't fall for you."

"I'll find another way," he repeated. "Besides, should you no' be protecting your employer?"

That drew her up short. Yes, she should. Any other time she would, but there had been something in Oscar's voice, something in the way he'd stared at her with those unusual gold eyes of his that night that had sent a warning through her.

"We looked for you," she said, rubbing the spot on her arm that Oscar had grabbed. "He wanted to meet you. He took me all over as we searched."

Sebastian's topaz eyes burned with anger as he sat up. "Did he hurt you?"

"He was...forceful. He's never laid a hand on me before. Not even a handshake. His reaction to you was unusual, but it was his treatment of me that makes me want to help you."

"You'll likely lose your job."

She thought about that and shrugged. "With my skills, I can get another."

"You doona understand," Sebastian said in a voice deepening with worry. "You know too much about Mikkel."

"Mikkel?" she asked with a frown. "You mean Oscar."

"Mikkel is his real name. Oscar is one of many aliases he uses."

It seemed it was a night of many eye-opening things. "I want to take your word for it, but—"

"You want proof," he said over her. "Unfortunately, giving you that information isna something I can do."

"Because of whatever it is you're part of, but don't want me involved in."

He gave a nod. "Trust me, you're better off."

Was she? She had never been an overcurious child. She was probably the only kid in the history of the world who didn't go snooping for her Christmas or birthday presents. She had somehow known that finding them would ruin things.

Why, then, did she feel the need to dig into Sebastian's past and discover whatever it was he was hiding, the thing that he kept pushing her away from—the thing that her employer seemed to be smack in the middle of?

"Stop thinking," Sebastian said.

She cut him a look. "I know every part of Oscar's schedule. I know where he was on any given day because I make the travel arrangements."

"Ah, lass, if only it were that easy. The many aliases, remember? Mikkel most likely has other personal assistants."

"But I traveled with him," she argued.

Sebastian put his hands behind him and leaned back. "All the time?"

"Well, no."

As she thought over the many times she was left behind, she began to have doubts about who her employer was. Perhaps she would do a bit of digging on her own. Oscar was gone anyway, and he'd never know.

"You need to forget everything I've told you," Sebastian said. "Once I leave—"

His words sent her heart dropping to her feet. "You're...leaving?"

He stared at her before he put a hand against her cheek. "I have to return to my family."

"When?" she persisted.

With his thumb caressing along her cheekbone, he tilted his head to the side. "Mikkel will be watching you closely. You need to resume your normal routine and never mention me. Doona ask him questions or pry into his life. If you do, he'll end yours without blinking."

She knew everything Sebastian said was right, but she couldn't get past the part about him leaving. It wasn't as if they were in a deep, committed relationship. She'd only met him and ended up in his bed a few days later.

Why, then, did she feel as if her world had just crashed around her?

And if she was going to lose him, she wasn't going to spend the remainder of whatever time she had left with Sebastian arguing about her employer.

She shoved his shoulder so that he fell back. She then straddled his hips and leaned over him, her hair falling like a curtain about his face.

He smiled, desire flashing in his eyes. "Ah, lass. I do love the way you think."

She kissed him and slid her sex over his hard cock. His groan sounded more like a growl, and it turned her on. Everything he did turned her on.

A gasp tore from her when she felt his arousal brush against her. "Condom," she mumbled as her desire heightened.

"I'm clean."

It was hard to think about being responsible when her body wanted him inside her so desperately.

He positioned his cock at her entrance. "I can no' get you with child," he said before he slipped inside her.

As soon as he filled her, nothing else mattered. She sat up and braced her hands on his chest as she began to rock her hips. Her head fell back when his hands cupped her breasts and began to knead them.

Just as before, there was no slow build. The fervor between them was cataclysmic, almost violent. There was no foreplay, no teasing—only the driving, compelling need to find ecstasy in each other's arms.

His hands on her hips urged her faster. She opened her eyes and looked at the ceiling, but she didn't see the thick wooden beams. She was blinded to everything except for Sebastian.

The desire grew tight and heavy in her belly, surging through her with a force she couldn't contain. Her lips parted as the orgasm ripped through her, taking her breath even as it filled her with warmth and spine-tingling rapture.

She heard Sebastian whisper something in a language she didn't understand right before he climaxed. Their bodies spent, she collapsed atop of him with his heartbeat in her ear.

Her eyes grew heavy. She didn't fight the pull of sleep, but welcomed it. As she began to drift off, his hand smoothed down her hair.

"I'm dangerous for you," he said.

She was awake enough to mumble, "I know."

If he said anything after, she didn't know because sleep had claimed her. When she next woke, she was in the same position atop him, with her stomach rumbling. She lifted her head to find him smiling sleepily at her.

"Food?" he asked.

"Food," she said.

She wrapped a blanket around her as they walked from the bedroom and down the stairs, stepping over their discarded clothes and shoes.

The palazzo took her breath away. It was pure in style and classic in form. The muted colors accented with wood stained a subdued deep brown made each room feel warm and welcoming.

There were still items that one would expect in such a Venetian palace. Like the delightful frescoes adorning the walls, rugs that looked to date back to the seventeenth century in style, and classic furniture.

Yet there were modern conveniences as well. There was a state-of-the-art sound system that reached each room with cleverly hidden speakers she had to search to find. And the kitchen was a chef's dream, with everything anyone would ever need or want.

She climbed upon a barstool before the large island in the kitchen as he walked to the refrigerator. She looked around, finding that there wasn't a single thing she would change. The colors, the style, the lighting, and even the furniture was simple and elegant, though leaning more toward the masculine.

Her gaze returned to Sebastian to find him watching her with a lopsided grin. "This place suits you."

"Does it?" he asked as he began slicing cheese.

"It does indeed. How often are you here?"

He shrugged as he did a quick glance around. "No' as often as we probably should."

Gianna had been around families with money, the kind of money she suspected Sebastian was from. Those kinds of people rarely had only two residences. "How many houses does your family have?"

He paused and looked up, their eyes meeting. "What makes you think we have more than two?"

"Have you forgotten who I work for and the circles he runs in? I'm used to being around billionaires and millionaires. The fact you don't want to answer me makes me think you have several."

"We do," he said offhandedly and returned to the cheese. He handed her a slice. "Why does it matter?"

She laughed and held out her arms. "Look at this place. It's magnificent. I've been in some grand places, but this palazzo should be used more often with its views."

He turned and brought out a bottle of wine and two glasses. Then he moved to a cabinet and took out a jar of olives before getting a loaf of bread.

She waited until he was sitting beside her at the island with the food and wine between them before she said, "Your other properties must be even more gorgeous if they keep you from here."

"Work keeps me busy," he said and popped an olive in his mouth.

It was obvious by the way he was being so evasive that he really didn't want her to know of his family or whatever had brought him to Venice that involved Oscar. She knew he was probably right. She should leave it alone and go on with her life. But she couldn't. Whether it was the passion that held her captive, or something much deeper, she couldn't walk away from him or any of it.

"Have you seen Ulrik?" she asked.

He hesitated, as if he was unsure about what to say.

Then it hit her. "Oh, my God. He was the man at the masquerade. The one you stopped and stared at for a time."

"Gianna, please."

She leaned forward to look at him. "You wanted to find him, and you did."

"It isna that simple," Sebastian said.

She tore off a piece of bread and brought it to her lips. "Then explain it to me."

Chapter Thirteen

Sebastian's gaze was on Gianna's lips as her tongue peeked out and licked away a crumb of bread. Damn but the woman had him in a knot of desire that wouldn't loosen.

"Well?" she pressed in his silence.

He drained the rest of his wine and set aside the empty glass. If he didn't give her something, she'd never stop asking. "Think of Ulrik as banished."

Gianna's brows rose high on her forehead. "Banished? What did he do?"

"I didna stand beside him," Sebastian said, ignoring her question. "None of us did."

She finished chewing and swallowing. "Would anything have changed had you stood with him?"

"Maybe. I'll never know."

"Why didn't you?"

Sebastian popped a slice of cheese into his mouth and considered her words as he chewed. "Ulrik had been in a downward spiral. He needed something that would jerk him out of it, to see how things were."

"And did it work?"

"No' as we'd hoped. He...got worse."

She wiped her hands as she finished the snack. "I might better understand if you'd tell me what happened."

There was no way he could tell her any of it without spilling everything. He'd already made Mikkel take special notice of her.

Sebastian wouldn't put her in any more danger.

He took her hand and pulled her from the stool as he stood. Then he tugged her after him up the stairs to the master bath. He turned on the water in the shower, and as it heated, he removed the blanket from around her.

She smiled and walked into his arms. Staring into her eyes, he knew that he'd made a dreadful mistake in using her. Not only because of Mikkel's interest, but because he hadn't cared about her feelings. He'd thought only about himself and Ulrik and not about how his actions could hurt others.

In the time he'd spent with Gianna, he'd discovered that she mattered to him. He cared for her and about her. When she'd stopped being an object to get to what he wanted, Sebastian wasn't sure. And it no longer signified. He'd stepped over that invisible line—and there was no going back.

"Sebastian?" she asked with a growing frown.

He pushed open the glass door of the shower and drew her with him as he stepped inside. He closed them in as steam filled the area. The hot water fell over them from both shower heads on either wall. He watched her eyes fall shut as she leaned her head back to wet her hair. Her breasts thrust out, her nipples forming hard little points as the water sluiced over them.

He didn't want the night to end, but already the sun was creeping close to the horizon. He'd already made his decision to leave Venice. Though he didn't have definitive proof, he'd seen enough with his own eyes to know. That should be enough to convince Con to move forward with an investigation. At least Sebastian hoped it was enough.

He lathered his hands with soap and began to wash Gianna, massaging her muscles as he did. He took his time, touching every part of her before slowly rinsing her body. Her seductive smile as she grabbed the soap from him made his cock twitch. He stood still as stone while she cleaned him. It wasn't until she came to his cock that he grabbed the wall.

His head fell back as her mouth covered him. He couldn't get enough of her. The more he kissed and touched, the more he thrust inside her, the more of her he had to have.

He took her in the shower.

He took her on the bathroom floor.

He took her against the door.

Somehow they made it back to the bed, where he took her twice more.

They dozed and ate between the lovemaking, not caring that the sun rose to its zenith and began its decent again. It was just the two of them in a world of ecstasy and desire, a world where no one else existed.

They made love in each room of the palazzo amid chases and laughter. There was no more talk of Ulrik, Mikkel, or their pasts. It was only about pleasure.

After a quick meal of strawberries and whipped cream, he'd set her on the island and spread her legs to feast upon her once more.

That was an hour ago. Now they were in the oversized tub filled with steaming water. He wrapped his arms around her as she rested back against him. Both had been silent, because they knew their time was coming to an end.

She lifted her hand from the water, raising her arm to watch the droplets run down her limb. "I wish I could stop time."

"I know," he murmured and kissed the side of her face. "I do as well."

"The day flew past. And why do I feel like everything is ending?"

Because it was, though he wouldn't tell her that. "It's no' over yet."

She reached back and wrapped her arms around him, a moan rumbling in her chest. "My body is no longer mine. You've touched every inch. I can feel you on my skin and deep inside me."

He brought her arms down before running his hand along her arm and intertwining their fingers. His mouth moved to her ear where he whispered, "I can still feel your fire."

"It'll always be yours."

They remained until the water began to cool. It was the only thing that drove them from their silence. Sebastian glanced out the window and saw the darkness. He knew before Gianna finished drying off that she was leaving.

His mind raced with ideas of how he could get her to stay. He started to reach for her, to kiss her and make love to her again, but it was only prolonging the inevitable. He had business he needed to take care of, and the farther away Gianna was from that, the better.

While she gathered her clothes in the trail they'd left, he grabbed a pair of jeans and a white tee. When he went downstairs barefoot, he found her sitting on the sofa putting on her shoes.

His boat had been returned last night, thanks to his careful planning and the huge amount of money he'd paid. He could drive her home, but Sebastian knew he wouldn't leave her if he did. The best thing would be to let her go now. Though it was killing him.

She drew in a deep breath and released it as she came to her feet. "This is good-bye, isn't it?"

"It is."

Her eyes moved to look out the windows over the Grand Canal. "But you'll return one day."

"Sure," he lied. He didn't have the courage to give her the entire truth—that as long as she was alive, he'd never return to Venice.

Because if he did, he'd go to her.

He'd search until he found her—and then he'd never let her go again.

Because of that, he'd never return. How could he when he'd be bombarded with thoughts of his Ice Queen who burned with a fire that had singed his very soul?

There was no denying she could be his mate, but he wouldn't be selfish and bring her into the middle of a war where the outcome could go either way.

"Come," he said and took her hand.

He walked her to the dock, where he flagged down a *topetta*. As it made its way to them, Sebastian drew her into his arms and kissed her. It was meant as a farewell, but at her taste, he wasn't able to hold back his longing, his hunger...or his regret.

Gianna was the one who ended the kiss and pulled out of his arms. She smiled softly and lightly touched his jaw with her fingers. "Thank you."

He stood, warring with himself, his heart bellowing for him to make her stay, as she climbed into the boat. His soul gave up a sorrowful cry that only he could hear—and feel—as the *topetta* drove away.

While he watched her, his mind drifted to Mikkel. It was Sebastian's hope that Mikkel would soon realize he was gone and Gianna was innocent. But what if Mikkel didn't? What if she got into trouble? What if Mikkel harmed her?"

Sebastian turned on his heel and made his way back into the palazzo. Once there, he found the mobile Ryder made him bring and rang Gianna's house. He waited for the answering machine to pick up, then he left her his number. "In case you need anything," he said before he disconnected the line.

He already missed her, and he feared that his feelings wouldn't lessen with time. A part of him wanted to go after her, to tell her everything about the Dragon Kings, Ulrik, and Mikkel, but he didn't.

As other Kings had brought women to Dreagan, Sebastian always thought of Ulrik. All of this had begun because Ulrik had fallen in love. They were in the middle of a war with the Dark Fae, Mikkel, and most likely Ulrik, all because Ulrik had dared to love.

Con feared that history was doomed to repeat itself, that a human would betray a King again. That's not what kept Sebastian from reaching out to Gianna.

He let her go because he knew she was better off without him and the war surrounding him. It was a war she knew nothing about, a war the Kings had gone to great lengths to keep from the humans. But how much longer would that work?

The farther away Gianna was from him, the better she'd be. She could continue her life without knowing about the Dragon Kings, Fae, Druids, or Warriors. She could keep looking at the world without knowing how magic lived and breathed alongside her—and not be in danger because of it.

He braced his hands on the island and hung his head as grief flooded him. His lungs refused to work as an ache filled his chest that threatened to send him to his knees. He squeezed his eyes closed as his throat clogged with emotion so volatile that he nearly shifted right then.

Somehow, he reined in his emotions, but nothing could stop the pain in his heart. Getting over Gianna was going to be the toughest thing he'd ever attempt, and he knew she was the one he'd never get past. She had seeped into his very psyche and effortlessly become part of his world. He'd come to Venice to use her, to get information on Mikkel, and instead, her fiery passion had engulfed him, flayed him.

And renewed him.

Sebastian pushed away from the island and began cleaning the kitchen. He had to do something to fill the time or he would do something stupid like go after her. He washed and dried the dishes and wiped off the counters. Then he made his way upstairs.

In the bedroom, he stood at the foot of the bed, staring at it, remembering how Gianna had felt in his arms. How her cries of pleasure had been music to his ears. How he loved watching the ecstasy pass over her face every time she climaxed.

He turned his back to the bed and clenched his teeth, that wickedly painful emotion threatening to make him shift again. Then he picked up his discarded clothes from the night before, hanging them back in the closet to be picked up later for cleaning.

With a vicious yank, he stripped the bed of the sheets and tossed them into a pile for the maids. Then he cleaned their mess in the bathroom, anything to keep him busy and his mind from Gianna. Except everywhere he looked, he saw her, smelled her.

Felt her.

He was walking through the rooms to look for anything he missed when he spotted their masks on the table near the sofa sitting side by side.

His knees buckled as he fell to the floor. How had he missed them when he walked her out? But he knew. He'd been too focused on her and saying good-bye. She'd left hers behind on purpose, of that he was sure.

With his jaw clenched, he reached for them, his hand shaking. He brought hers against his chest and held it, imagining it was her. Then, somehow, he climbed to his feet and made his way upstairs to the closet. He opened the cabinet where the other masks were and returned his to its rightful place. Then he set hers below his.

It sparkled, just as she did—and always would.

He ran his fingers over it, recalling how stunning she'd looked, how free. And her smile. It had dazzled.

Sebastian dropped his hand and closed the cabinet door, shutting away the masks and the memories. As he walked back into the bedroom, he opened the mental link all dragons had and called Con's name.

The King of Kings answered a short time later. "*Aye.*"

"*I have proof.*"

Con sighed. "*Definitive?*"

"*I saw Mikkel. And I saw Ulrik.*"

"*Together?*" Con asked brusquely.

Sebastian sank into a chair near the fireplace. "*Nay. It was Mikkel's ball. He's using the name Oscar Cox here in Venice. But Ulrik was there in full masquerade costume.*"

"Then how did you know it was Ulrik?"

"The same way you would've. It's his eyes. And...he spoke to me."

"What did he say?"

"He told me that I put Gianna's life at risk. He told me to leave Venice before it was too late."

"Do you believe he was threatening her or you?" Con asked.

"I think he was warning me."

There was a moment of silence, then Con said, *"Did you see Mikkel's face?"*

"He had on a half mask, but I saw enough. He looks almost identical to Ulrik. The only difference is the gray at his temples. Just like the photo Ryder found."

"Come home. It's time we decide how to proceed."

"Since I can no' return in dragon form, I must wait for my flight that departs in the morning."

"Hurry," Con said before severing the link.

Sebastian stalked from the bedroom. He'd sleep in the boat below the palazzo. It was the only way he'd get any sort of peace.

If any existed for him beyond that point now that Gianna was gone.

Chapter Fourteen

Memories were a way to relive a certain time. And Gianna was holding onto hers with both hands. It was those memories that would remind her of who she was, of who Sebastian helped her become.

Her heart was broken, shattered. Crushed. Yet there were no tears. The pain was too raw, too visceral. All of it was so new, but it would wear off, and when it did, that's when the tears would hit her.

It was inevitable after coming in contact with such a vibrant, masculine man who evoked images of primal, untamed warriors who conquered all in their path. And he had conquered her. Easily and smoothly. Not even knowing that the pain of his departure was going to destroy her did she regret any of it.

With Sebastian she discovered a great passion, the kind she had long believed would never be hers. She felt what it was to be adored and her body worshipped. So no matter the pain—and it was going to strike deep—she embraced what had happened.

When she'd returned home to find his message, she had listened to it over a dozen times. And she would never delete it. Because that voice of his was a slice of heaven she'd turn to when the times got tough.

Even though she didn't expect to ever call him, she programmed his number simply with the letter S. Having his number was a cruel sort of torture that she planned to carry around with her always, but then again, she couldn't seem to help herself when it came to Sebastian.

The morning began with a long shower before she stood in front of her open closet. It wasn't that she had a difficult time finding something to wear. It was that she didn't see any of her clothes. Her mind kept drifting back to the day before when Sebastian had made love to her multiple ways with his tender touch and hot mouth.

Finally, she chose a cream sweater dress with a V-neck that hugged her curves and came down just below her kneecaps. She added a belt in saddle brown and nude heels.

When it came time for her hair, she was going to leave it down, but she changed her mind and pulled it back into her traditional bun. She skipped breakfast and grabbed her cream trench coat and purse on the way out the door.

As she stood in front of the office building, she had to make herself go inside and up to her office. She didn't know if Oscar Cox was Mikkel or not, but she no longer wanted any part of him or his business.

Once she was in her office, she found a list of things she had to take care of. Phone calls to return and emails to answer. She sat down and immediately got to work. It was a small reprieve for her mind away from Sebastian and the mystery surrounding Mikkel and Ulrik.

Sometime during the night, she had stopped thinking of her employer as Oscar and began calling him Mikkel. It was something she would have to watch whenever she spoke to him, but she didn't foresee that being a problem, since she intended to quit.

She finished responding to the majority of the emails and was on a phone call when her cell phone buzzed. After she completed jotting down notes, she reached for her cell as she was ending the call.

As soon as Gianna saw it was from Oscar, her stomach dropped to her feet. She hung up the phone and stared at the message for a long time. It wasn't as if it were odd for Mikkel to call her to the palazzo if they were discussing plans for a party, but since one had just occurred, it wasn't like him to already plan another in the same location. That could only mean he wanted to talk about other things.

Besides, he was supposed to have left Venice last night.

Well, he was going to be sorely disappointed, because she wasn't going to be there.

She checked the clock to see it was another two hours before their meeting. Gianna quickly wrote up her resignation letter, printed and signed it before she rose and walked to put it on his desk.

Whoever Mikkel might be, he had no right to pry into her personal life. Just because she worked for him didn't give him those kinds of privileges.

She grabbed her cream trench coat and belted it in place before she picked up her purse and left the office without a backward glance. There would be enough time for her to get into Mikkel's palazzo and have a look around before her resignation went into effect thirty minutes before their meeting. She'd dated and added the time specifically for that reason.

Not that any of it would matter. She would have come and gone from the palazzo, changed her cell number, and been in the middle of looking for another apartment all before Mikkel even knew what happened.

If she were really lucky, she'd find some evidence to help Sebastian. Though in the back of her mind, she knew she was looking for an excuse to see him again.

On the boat ride to the palazzo, there was a voice in her head urging her not to go, to head straight for her house. That voice was so loud and insistent that when they docked at the palazzo, she hesitated in getting off.

Then she thought of Sebastian and how much he wanted to bring his brother back to the family. He hadn't gotten anything on his trip, and this was her chance to give him what he'd set out for.

She paid the driver and stepped from the boat. The palazzo was quiet as she unlocked the door and entered. Without the glittering lights, brightly dressed guests, and loud music, it seemed as if she stepped into another world.

Everything had been returned to order the day before, making her doubt she had even been there for the masquerade. She softly closed the door and walked farther inside. Her first destination was the back room that Mikkel used for his office. It had a magnificent view of the Grand Canal.

Her shoes were quiet on the rugs as she approached the office. She tested the handle on the door to find it unlocked, then she pushed open the door. Once inside she looked at the bookshelves, where priceless works of art sold by Venetian families during restorations or financial hardships now sat. She was looking at things with a different perspective now, and she wasn't sure what to think.

Nor did she know what she needed to look for as she walked to the desk and began opening drawers. There was something there that would help Sebastian, she was sure of it.

"Now this is something I didn't expect to see."

She froze at Mikkel's voice and lifted her head to find him leaning casually against the doorframe with his hands in his pockets. Various responses ran through her head, but she remained quiet as she closed the drawer she'd been searching and straightened.

"Nothing to say?" Mikkel asked. He gave a shake of his head and glanced at the floor before pushing away from the door. "Our meeting isn't for a while yet. What are you doing here?"

He appeared to be alone, but she knew that he wasn't. Mikkel never went anywhere by himself. She calculated the odds of her getting out alive, and they were falling rapidly.

"Come, Gianna," he urged. "It's not like you to be so silent."

She raised her chin. He would know if she was lying, so she immediately shoved aside all the falsehoods that came to mind. Instead, she opted for the truth. "I was looking for something."

His brows rose as he gave her a look of approval and slowly came toward her. "The truth. How novel."

She began to back away, moving around the other side of the desk. Once cleared of it, she would have a direct path from the office to the front door.

Mikkel reached his desk and ran his fingers along the top. "I trusted you."

"And I trusted you."

"When did he get to you?"

The time for truth was over. There was no way she was going to tell him anything about Sebastian. "Who?"

"Don't play dumb," he admonished. "It doesn't suit you."

She squared her shoulders. "I don't know what you're talking about."

"The man at my ball." Mikkel steepled his fingers on his desk and looked at her. "He's the reason you're here."

"You think you know the answers, when in fact you don't."

He straightened in mock surprise. "Then, please, by all means, enlighten me."

If only she had an answer. Her mind was completely blank. There wasn't anything plausible she could come up with. Not one single response. Of all the times for her mind to be empty, now was extremely inconvenient.

"That's what I thought," Mikkel said.

"I choose not to answer because you wouldn't believe anything I said."

He shrugged one shoulder indifferently. "As much as this game intrigues me, I find myself impatient."

"For?" she asked when he grew silent.

The smile that formed was one of pure evil, filled with malice and brutality that made her blood turn to ice. That voice from earlier that had warned her away from the palazzo was saying "I told you so." Very loudly.

"Call him," Mikkel demanded.

She frowned and glanced behind her to find the doorway still empty. "Who?"

"You know who. There's no telling what name he used. He changes them often enough. I'm talking about the man you were seen with at the masquerade. Call him." His smile vanished, replaced with a sneer of malevolence. "Now!"

She jumped at his barked order. The unspoken threat of bodily harm hung in the air, making her shake. Her heart slammed against her rib cage.

It took her two tries before she found her voice. Even then, it came out shaky. "I don't know who you're talking about."

His smile was tight as he came around the desk. She backed up a step and spun around, ready to run. Only to come to a halt when she saw the two men at the door.

Gianna turned to face Mikkel. He halted two feet from her and shook his head slowly as he looked her up and down. She didn't know what was going on in his mind, but she knew that if she got out of this situation, she was going to get as far from Venice as she could.

"I learned early on that humanity couldn't be trusted," Mikkel said. "How easily you are swayed. It's true that everyone has their price. It's surprising how low some of those are."

She shifted so she could keep an eye on Mikkel and his two goons at the door. "I don't have a price."

"Sure you do," he stated. "For the majority, I offer them money and they take it, agreeing to do whatever it is I want. There are the few who hold out. That is, until I threaten their lives. Those fold pretty quickly. Then there are the rare ones, the ones like you, Gianna. The ones who make me threaten their families."

She might not get along with her father, but that didn't mean she wanted him killed. Damn. He knew just how to get to her.

Mikkel watched her. "You see, I learn people. Because, inevitably, I have to intimidate them. I thought you might be the exception, but I was wrong. I always knew if this moment ever came that I had only one play—your father."

She swallowed, the sound loud in the silence. Without even realizing how, she'd found herself between a rock and a hard place— with no escape in sight.

"You need to understand that I'm not bluffing," Mikkel said. He took a step closer. "One of my men is in New York right now with a gun aimed through the window of your father's apartment, waiting for me to give the order. The decision is yours. Will you kill your father?"

"You're a bastard."

He shrugged, twisting his lips. "I see the defiance in your gaze. I'll give you a warning I don't normally share with others. I always win. Always. There's nothing you can do or say that will surprise me. That's because I've thought of every angle." He closed the space between them so that she leaned back to get away from him. "Now call my nephew."

Gianna searched for a lie in his words, something that would tell her that she could get out of this, that she and Sebastian could beat him.

But there was nothing.

She pulled her phone out of her purse and found Sebastian's contact. Then she pressed the button to call him. She was shaking uncontrollably as she brought the phone to her ear, her gaze locked with Mikkel's.

Sebastian answered in the middle of the second ring. "Gianna?"

"Hi," she said, her chest heaving.

There was a slight pause. Then he asked, "What happened? Tell me what's wrong."

Mikkel smiled in triumph. "Tell him to come here."

She wished she had the courage to tell Mikkel no, to destroy her cell phone and hit him hard enough to knock him out. But she didn't. She was terrified and anxious, her fear knotting tightly in her gut.

"Gianna?" Sebastian said through the phone.

She fought back tears of dread and panic, her throat tightening as the feelings welled higher. "I need you to come to the palazzo."

"I see," Sebastian replied in a soft, calm voice.

The line disconnected. As she lowered the cell phone, Mikkel knocked it out of her hand and backed her against the wall.

"You're in for quite a show, my dear."

Chapter Fifteen

Sebastian hung up the phone and set it on the bed as dread and anger began to churn inside him. He'd heard the fear in Gianna's words. The way her voice wobbled was enough to send him into a rage. He didn't need to ask her to know that Mikkel had gotten to her. Or was it Ulrik? Or worse—both?

Even though he'd told Con he had proof about Mikkel, since he'd seen Ulrik at the ball, Sebastian couldn't stop thinking that maybe Con was right. Maybe Ulrik was a part of all of it. That could be why Ulrik wouldn't talk to him at the ball.

Not that it mattered. Gianna was being used to get to him. And Sebastian didn't like to disappoint. Not to mention, he was ready for a fight.

He rose, thinking of the Dark Fae he'd seen at the party. They would be waiting for him. Quite frankly, he was more than ready to kill some Dark. The fuckers seemed to find their way into every nook and cranny.

Con needed to know what was happening, but Sebastian knew if he spoke with Con that the King of Kings would ask him to wait until another King could arrive. That was time Sebastian couldn't give him.

He looked down at the mobile phone on the bed. Since Sebastian couldn't call Con on the mobile or use their mental link, he sent a text instead. Then dropped the phone on the bed before he walked out to find Gianna.

He strode down the street to the palazzo. People were everywhere, but he paid them no mind. His thoughts were on Gianna and what awaited him. The hope that she would be kept in the dark about his secrets was shot. Mikkel would likely tell her everything. After all Sebastian had done to keep the truth from her, and she was going to find out anyway. It infuriated him.

And saddened him.

By the time he reached the palazzo, he was ready for battle. He watched the door for a few minutes before he walked to it. Not bothering to knock, he threw it open and waited for an attack.

But none came.

Something was wrong. He couldn't put his finger on it, but someone should've been at the entrance. No doubt Mikkel had a surprise waiting for him somewhere else.

Sebastian entered the house with slow steps. He used his enhanced hearing and eyesight to his advantage, but there was nothing to see in the shadows where the sunlight didn't reach. More troubling was that the house was as quiet as a tomb.

When he entered the main foyer, he turned his head to the side and saw a female Dark who was filing her nails. She looked up, spearing him with blood red eyes. She sighed with boredom and flipped her long length of black and silver hair over her shoulder.

"I was beginning to wonder if you were coming," she said in an Irish accent.

He glanced around, waiting for more Dark to attack. "Where is the girl?"

The Dark rolled her eyes as she dropped her hands to her side. "Follow the trail."

"That's all you have to say?"

She issued another loud sigh. "I was told to give you that message. No one said anything about fighting, and I'm not stupid enough to challenge a Dragon King."

And with that, she teleported away.

Sebastian wanted to take that as a good sign, but he knew better. "Follow the trail," he mumbled.

What trail? He turned in a circle, not seeing anything. Then he caught a whiff of something he knew all too well. The sweet, coppery smell of blood.

He jerked his head in its direction and hurried into the office. When he saw the drops of blood, he knew they were Gianna's. And just as the Dark had told him, there was a trail—of blood.

Hands clenched into fists, he followed the drops to a wall. Since he knew Gianna couldn't walk through walls, it had to be a hidden door. Frustration mounted as he took precious minutes to find the latch, which turned out to be a painting he needed to tilt to the side.

When the door slid open, he looked into the dark, narrow passage where his enemies lay in wait for him. Many of the old homes in Venice had such secret tunnels. He didn't hesitate to enter and follow the blood. His steps were measured, slow. There were five different offshoots of the main passage, but the trail didn't deviate. By the slope of the floor, he was descending beneath the palazzo.

After what felt like an eternity, the tunnel ended before a door. No one had stopped him. No one had been waiting for him. But that would surely change now. He could hear voices on the other side of the wooden door. As soon as he detected the Irish accents, he peeled back his lips and kicked the door in.

The wood splintered as the two male Dark jerked in surprise. Sebastian strode through the busted door and grabbed the nearest Fae, slamming his head into the stone wall.

Sebastian ducked an orb of magic thrown by the second Fae. Then he rushed the Dark with a growl, wrapping his hands around the male's throat and squeezing it until the spinal column snapped.

He ripped the hearts out of both Dark just to be sure they were dead. His bloodlust tempered with the demise of such evil creatures and allowed the band around his heart to ease some. He took a deep breath and picked up the trail of blood again.

No doubt more Dark would attack him, but he was ready. Mikkel was doing his best to make it difficult for him to find Gianna. Why? Mikkel was the one who wanted him. If the bastard hoped to throw him off by making him trudge through the narrow passage, he was going to be in for a surprise.

Sebastian moved through the low-ceilinged rooms, each one growing larger and larger as the ground steadily inclined. He was being taken back to the surface. To what, though? Obviously it was a trap. But to what end?

He clenched his teeth together. Mikkel was bringing him someplace private, somewhere humans wouldn't stumble upon them. And that was bad news for Gianna.

As Sebastian walked, the drops of blood became redder, fresher, signaling he was getting close. Finally, he passed through one last doorway and found himself in the middle of a large room stacked with crates.

His gaze landed on Mikkel, who had Gianna pulled back against him, his fingers wrapped around her throat tightly. Rage swelled within him at the way Mikkel was handling her. The dripping of the blood from a cut on her finger only enraged him more.

"I'm here," he stated.

"You've got to be fucking joking," Mikkel spat in a British accent. "What are you doing here, Sebastian?"

If there had been any last doubt about who Mikkel was, it was gone. But it was his surprise that shocked Sebastian. Just who had he thought was coming? "I'm looking for you."

"Me?" Mikkel asked with a bark of laughter. "You mean Ulrik."

Sebastian shook his head. "I mean you."

It was the narrowing of Mikkel's gaze that alerted Sebastian his statement didn't sit well. Mikkel's surprise meant only one thing—he'd made sure to keep his identity from the Kings. Any dragon would've been drawn to Dreagan because of the magic there, but not Mikkel. The fact he stayed away was telling. And troubling. Mikkel had to be dealt with—now.

Sebastian wanted to demand that Mikkel release Gianna, but he didn't. To do so would let Mikkel know how much she meant to him. No matter how much Sebastian wanted to kill him, he had to get Gianna away safely.

"Why don't we get on with this?" Sebastian asked. "You called me here for a reason."

Mikkel's face hardened in anger. "Where's Ulrik? Tell him to come out."

Now, wasn't that an interesting development? Sebastian had come to Venice to prove that Mikkel was the one the Kings should be after, not Ulrik. And Mikkel had all but admitted he was acting alone by his words.

"Where's Ulrik?" Mikkel shouted.

Sebastian shrugged and looked around. "How am I supposed to know?"

Mikkel laughed harshly. "I knew Ulrik would never be able to stand against Con. No' before when he was King. No' now."

The Scots brogue came out loud and clear as Mikkel raged, when he'd been so careful with his British accent before. Sebastian filed that away for later. "You think I'm here with Ulrik?"

"Of course," Mikkel said, spittle flying. "No' that it matters. I've got something special planned for all of you."

Gianna elbowed Mikkel in the side and attempted to get away. He yanked her back by the bun, causing her to cry out in pain.

Sebastian watched it all helplessly, silently raging and planning all kinds of agony for Mikkel. Before Gianna's attempted escape, Mikkel's attention had been on him. Now he was focused on her. Exactly what Sebastian hadn't wanted.

"What about her?" Mikkel asked as he tugged hard on her hair.

Gianna's face pinched with discomfort and she grabbed his hand in an effort to minimize the pain.

Sebastian kept his gaze off Gianna, though it was one of the hardest things he'd ever done. "What about her? She's only a mortal."

"You don't expect me to believe that, do you?" Mikkel asked with a raised brow. "All of you Dragon Kings love to tell the women you bring to your beds who you are."

"That's no' true."

Mikkel looked between him and Gianna before he began laughing. "Ah, so you kept it from her. How fascinating. Why?"

"It's no' her business," Sebastian stated.

Mikkel wrenched her head back and peered into her face. "Did you hear that? That means you weren't important enough."

Sebastian noted his English accent was back in place. "It means she didna need to be involved."

"But you did involve her." Mikkel looked at him. "You're the one who is responsible for this. For her knowing...everything."

Sebastian had known it would come to this. "This is between us."

"I'm afraid not. This is so much bigger than us." He walked to the left, half-dragging Gianna behind him.

Sebastian watched as she twisted an ankle trying to keep up with Mikkel. Strands of her hair loosened from her bun and fell about her, green eyes silently cried out for him to help. More than anything he wanted to get her from Mikkel's grasp, but to attempt it would most likely bring about her death. So he remained still, watching them.

"Why no' bring a human into it?" Mikkel asked, his voice raised as the brogue returned. He viciously slung Gianna against a stack of crates and released his hold on her. "The mortals were there to begin with. I think it's fitting one be with us now."

Sebastian took a slow step toward them. "Enough."

"No' nearly." Mikkel bent and put his face next to Gianna's in her position on the floor. "Did you know your lover is immortal? A Dragon King?"

Gianna looked from Mikkel to him, but Sebastian didn't reply. There was nothing to say.

Mikkel laughed and straightened. "Let me give you a brief history lesson, Gianna. This realm was ours. We dragons called this planet home for millions of years before you showed up."

Sebastian winced at the way her face lost all color.

"We had a chance to wipe you out," he continued. "But the King of Dragon Kings chose no' to."

"It wasna just Con," Sebastian stated.

Mikkel nodded, pressing his lips together. He clapped his hands once and went down on his haunches to be even with Gianna. "Listen close, mortal, there's going to be a test at the end. Every dragon clan had a King. The strongest, most powerful of that clan." He then pointed to Sebastian. "He is such a dragon."

Sebastian was fast losing patience. "Mikkel—"

"But even the Dragon Kings need to be controlled," Mikkel said over him. "A King of Kings. That is Constantine. You see, he and my nephew were as close as brothers. When the mortals arrived, all of the Kings were able to shift into human form to talk to them."

"To make peace," Sebastian interjected.

Mikkel gave a loud snort. "When we should've showed them who ruled, no' moved dragons away from lands they'd had for centuries just so the fucking humans could settle."

"You didna like that, did you?" he guessed.

Mikkel swung his head to him. "No one did."

"But you had to listen to your King. You had to listen to Ulrik."

"He should never have been King!" Mikkel exploded as he stood.

And that's when the truth hit Sebastian with the force of a meteor. "You instigated the war."

Mikkel's smile was slow and vile. "Bravo, King. I'm almost sad you're going to have to die."

Chapter Sixteen

Dreagan

Con's head jerked up from the papers he was looking over at his desk as Ryder threw open the door to his office. The look of shock and consternation on Ryder's face had Con softly setting down his Montblanc pen as he prepared himself for whatever news was about to be dropped.

"What is it?" he asked.

Ryder walked into the office and stopped before the desk. He held out a mobile phone. Con frowned as he looked from Ryder to the device.

"Read it," Ryder urged.

Con took the mobile and read over Sebastian's text twice. Con slowly got to his feet as the hot coals of anger flared to life. "Thirteen words? 'He has Gianna. He wants me. I'm going to take care of this.' Who is Sebastian talking about?"

Ryder shrugged. "It could be Ulrik. It could be Mikkel."

"Dammit," Con said and tossed Ryder the phone before he crushed it in his fury. "When did that come through?"

"Just now."

"Which means Bast sent it right before he went to meet whoever it is."

Ryder lifted a brow and nodded. "That's what I'd do if I wanted to keep everyone out of it."

"Me as well," Con admitted grudgingly.

"It's out of our hands now."

And that's what pissed Con off the most. "Patience isna something I possess, especially in this instance. Find Lily and Denae. See which one wants to fly me back to Venice."

"You could go yourself."

After he'd grounded all the dragons, Con wasn't going to shift and fly to Venice in his true form when none of the others could. Though it killed his soul each time he had to fly in the damn helicopters or planes.

"But you willna," Ryder said into the silence.

Con walked around his desk. "I want to leave in the next fifteen minutes."

"There's no time for that."

He halted and looked at Ryder. "What do you mean?"

"It'll take hours to get to Venice. Hours you can no' allow to pass. You can make it there in less than half the time."

Con knew it was true, but still he hesitated. As the minutes ticked by, he thought of Ulrik fighting Sebastian. Did Ulrik know Bast had gone to Venice to help him? The idea of Ulrik killing Sebasatian was what finally made Con's decision.

"Find Bast. I want to know exactly where he is by the time I reach Venice," Con said as he strode from his office to find Arian.

Using the secret door from the conservatory into the mountain attached to the manor, Con found Arian. He motioned Arian with him as he quickly relayed what was going on while they made their way to the back entrance to the mountain.

"I need a storm stretching from here to Italy," Con said as he removed his gold dragon-head cuff links before shrugging out of his jacket and taking off his dress shirt. His shoes and slacks were next.

Arian gave a nod as he used his power to create a storm. "Let me come with you."

"No' this time," Con said as thunder rumbled around them, shaking the ground. A moment later, lightning crashed.

Con shifted and allowed himself a moment to bask in the glory of being in his true form. The weeks he'd prohibited any shifting had had a profound effect on everyone—including him. The anxiety that had gripped him lessened now. He took a deep breath and stretched his wings.

It was all he could do not to barrel from the mountain and into the air, that's how strong his craving was to fly. And though he wouldn't admit it to anyone, he understood and accepted Ulrik's anger at not being able to shift.

He shoved those thoughts aside and walked to the large opening. He looked at the sky as fat raindrops began to fall. Then he spread his wings and jumped into the air. The first rush of wind over his wings made his heart catch and race with delight. He flew toward the clouds, enjoying every second.

But this exhilaration shouldn't be his alone. He looked down at Dreagan to see the other Kings standing outside watching. He didn't need to look at their faces to know they ached to take to the skies, that they longed to feel the wind around them.

He opened the link to all of them and said, *"Resume patrols around the perimeter of Dreagan. It's time we took back our land."*

No sooner had his words ended than each of the Kings shifted and began flying. He circled back once to see all of his brethren where they belonged—in the sky.

* * * *

Gianna shivered uncontrollably. The cold was sinking into her skin, but it was the brutality in Mikkel's voice that froze her. There was no doubt in her mind that he intended to kill Sebastian. As crazy as the things Mikkel was saying were, she wasn't going to stand by and watch her lover die.

"You're wrong," she blurted out.

Mikkel's head slowly turned to her as he raised a brow. "I'm wrong?"

"Yes."

He faced her and asked politely, "Which part?"

"All of it." She glanced at Sebastian to see him shaking his head, as if telling her to stop.

Mikkel began to laugh, softly at first, but then the sound grew louder. "Oh, that never gets old. You mortals think you know everything. In fact, you know nothing. You're like the spoiled, entitled, selfish brats I see all around me."

"There are no dragons," she insisted.

"There are two standing right before you." Mikkel's tone held a cruel edge to it as his gold eyes glowed with an intense light. "We walk around in these forms to blend in with you. But we've magic and powers you can't begin to fathom."

She lifted her chin. "Show me."

Mikkel swung his head to Sebastian. "Yes, why don't you show her, Sebastian? Too afraid she might run away screaming? That's what they all do."

"No' all," Sebastian stated.

Mikkel shrugged indifferently. "Most of them. There are a few who won't, whether from curiosity or stupidity, I can't say." He threw out his hands and smiled widely. "I know what will liven things up. Why don't we have more friends join our little party?"

Gianna must have hit her head earlier, because suddenly there were four more men in the room with them. They looked menacing, their attention on Sebastian. They each appeared similar, being clad in all black with various lengths of their black hair shot through with silver. Though their look was curious, there was an ominous cloud that hung over them.

Tension filled the air. The four men stood rigid, expectant. Sebastian, on the other hand, looked as if he would be happy to rip their heads off. As the seconds passed, the strain of impending battle stifled the air until it fairly vibrated with fury.

Mikkel squatted beside her, a gleeful smile in place. "Do you know who they are?"

"How would I?" She glanced at him, noting that he didn't seem affected by any of what she was witnessing. Perhaps that was because he was instigating all of it. The bastard.

"This is part of your lesson, so listen carefully," he warned as he leaned close. "Those are Fae. Dark Fae, to be exact. You can always tell a Dark because of the silver in their black hair as well as their red eyes." He wrinkled his nose and said offhandedly, "There are Light Fae as well, but they aren't nearly as fun."

She swallowed in alarm as she watched a swirling iridescent ball form in one of the men's hands. She blinked rapidly, hoping it was just a trick of the light or her eyes, but there was no denying what she was seeing. It made her reevaluate her thoughts on everything Mikkel was telling her—and how Sebastian had fought not to share anything with her before.

"What's that?" she asked softly. If she was going to watch this, then she wanted to know what she was looking at. And prepare herself both mentally and physically.

"Magic." Mikkel smiled and said, "If you hadn't already slept with Sebastian, I'd show you just what the Dark do to mortals. They would look at you, and you'd be on your knees stripping out of your clothes, begging them to take you. Human souls are what they feed on, and each time they have sex, they drain mortals like you of their souls. You'd die with a smile on your face, feeling nothing but pleasure. But having sex with a Dragon King seems to negate the effect the Dark have on humans."

She jerked away from him, disgusted at his words. She wanted to tell him he was a liar, but something stopped her. Perhaps it was the orbs that were forming in the other three men's hands. Perhaps it was the glimpse of red eyes that she got. Or it could be that she'd always known Sebastian was different from other men.

"Don't be like other mortals," Mikkel said. "Accept what's before you. The Fae are here. So are the Dragon Kings."

One of the men—Fae—lifted a ball to throw at Sebastian. It was four against one. Four with magic, and even if Sebastian had it as well, he was outnumbered. She thought fast, trying to come up with a way to pause everything. And then it hit her.

"Tell me more." She looked into Mikkel's gold eyes. "Tell me the entire story."

He studied her for a moment before he said, "Lads, wait a moment."

The four Fae grumbled but the orbs disappeared. She met Sebastian's gaze, but she couldn't tell what he was thinking. He looked bored with the Fae, as if they couldn't hurt him. But she wasn't so confident.

"You think by having me tell you the story that it will buy Sebastian time," Mikkel said.

She shrugged and rubbed her head, which still hurt from his pulling of her hair. "You want me to know the details. I'm asking you to tell me. We both win. You told me this planet was yours until the humans came. When was that?"

Mikkel stood and moved to sit on a nearby crate. "The date doesn't matter. What you should be concerned with is the day everything changed. Con and the other Dragon Kings shifted for the first time in order to speak to the mortals. All of us knew your kind were weaker. They had no magic. So the Kings made a vow to protect the humans out of some misguided charity. Then the Kings gave your race a place to live."

"That was kind of them."

He gave a snort. "Perhaps for your people. Not for mine. Your race breeds like rabbits. You take more and more land, destroying it in the process. You think of nothing but making your life easier, uncaring how it is you get those things or what lives might be damaged because of it."

"Unfortunately, you're right. But that isn't all of us," she argued.

Mikkel raised his brows. "You use electricity, yes? Gas? Petroleum? You drive in cars and boats, fly around in planes. Yes?"

"Yes," she said with a nod of her head.

"So you're all the same. While the human population began to grow, more and more land was taken from the dragons. Much to my shock, many of the Dragon Kings built villages on their land for the mortals, even mingling with them. Some, like my nephew, even took them as lovers."

"That's how two different races find peace."

Mikkel gave her a wry look. "While the humans hunted the smaller dragons for food?"

She glanced at Sebastian before she asked, "And did the dragons not eat any humans?"

"A few," Mikkel conceded. "What you don't understand is that we'd been ordered by our Kings to leave the humans alone. A couple of large dragons taking a mortal as a snack is much different than the humans hunting and killing smaller dragons."

"So you got angry and started a war?" she asked.

Mikkel twisted his lips as he looked up. "That I did."

"Tell her all of it," Sebastian ordered.

Gianna looked at her lover and said, "You tell me."

"No," Mikkel barked and glared at Sebastian. His lip curled in anger. "This is my story."

She rose to her knees before standing and moving to sit atop a crate. Her body ached from the rough handling, and her finger throbbed from the cut. She kept pressure on it to stop the bleeding. "Fine. You tell the story then," she told Mikkel.

He looked between her and Sebastian before he said, "Ulrik was a fool. He was just like his father and ruled with kindness and mercy when the dragons needed a firm hand like mine."

"You mean a cruel hand," Sebastian said.

Mikkel ignored him and continued. "I wanted to teach Ulrik a lesson. The idiot fell in love with a mortal and wanted to take her as his mate. A human," Mikkel said in disgust. "Mated to a Dragon King. The thought turned my stomach. But nothing I said reached Ulrik. He didn't care that his line would die out because no mortal had carried a child to term from a Dragon King. It didn't make a difference to him. So I befriended his intended, Nala."

Gianna saw the outrage on Sebastian's face as friction filled the room.

Mikkel waved his hand. "She was easy to sway. All mortals are. After a few lies, she readily believed anything I needed her to believe. After that, she was willing to do whatever I wanted. So, I ordered her to kill Ulrik on the night of her mating."

Revulsion filled Gianna. She couldn't understand how someone could care so little about another's life or his own family to do something so heinous.

"Your plan didn't work," Gianna said.

Mikkel met her gaze. "I knew if she tried, it would result in war. Somehow Con discovered her plan and cornered her with the rest of the Dragon Kings. Sebastian and the others killed her."

"What he isna telling you," Sebastian said. "Is that had Nala gone through the mating ceremony, she would've been immortal. All mates of Dragon Kings remain alive as long as the Kings do. Then there is the fact that only a Dragon King can kill another Dragon King. Nala wouldna have been able to kill Ulrik, but her betrayal would've broken him."

Mikkel laughed as he got to his feet. "None of that matters. I wanted the Kings to see how troublesome the humans were. I wanted the Kings to rain down dragon fire and wipe the mortals from this earth." His gaze swung to her. "I didn't get my wish then, but I will this time."

Chapter Seventeen

It angered Sebastian that he wasn't the one telling Gianna the story. The only upside was that he was discovering all the missing pieces, thanks to Mikkel's confession.

The four Dark Fae standing between him and Gianna were worrisome though. It would be just like Mikkel to turn the Fae on her. Gianna had no magic with which to counter them, leaving her vulnerable.

The one saving grace was that since she'd been in his bed, she would feel no draw to the Fae. Though none of the Kings knew how, once a woman slept with them, those women were immune to all Fae.

"Ulrik isna the same as he was," Sebastian said into the silence after Mikkel's statement. "Before, he would've forgiven you anything. Now...he'll kill you."

Mikkel laughed loudly, the sound bouncing off the walls. "Indeed, he'll try, but he won't win. Not even with the Kings as allies."

Sebastian inwardly shook his head. While Mikkel thought Ulrik had aligned with the Kings, Con believed Ulrik and Mikkel were a team. It was a fine mess they were in, but one he was going to clear up as soon as he got back to Dreagan.

"Ulrik began the first war upon humans," Mikkel said. "And he's going to bring about the second." He looked at Gianna then and smiled. "There was one thing my nephew did right. After he discovered Nala's murder, he was grief-stricken. That quickly turned to rage against his brethren—and then against the mortals when Con told him how Nala was going to betray him. Ulrik set out that very night and began razing villages to the ground."

Sebastian scoffed at his words. "Aye, Ulrik was furious. He'd loved Nala. He took her in his home. He protected her and her family. How did you expect he'd feel?"

"I wanted him to remember he was a Dragon King!" Mikkel bellowed, spittle flying from his mouth in his fit of rage. "We doona demean ourselves to take a human as a mate. Fuck them all you want, but only a dragon should be mated to a King."

"He wasna the only one taking a mortal as a mate," Sebastian argued.

Mikkel gave a long look to Gianna. "If I was so wrong, why did over half of the Kings side with Ulrik and begin the war?"

"They all came back to Con's side in the end. We watched enough dragons die."

"Because you didna let them fight! You told them to guard the mortals, so they allowed themselves to be killed!"

Sebastian swallowed past the painful lump once Mikkel's words faded. He looked at Gianna to find a deep frown in place, puzzlement filling her green eyes. She didn't know what to believe. And how could she? He'd kept all of it from her.

"The blood of every dragon that died is on your hands. It's on the hands of every King." Mikkel gave a snort, his face contorted with loathing. "Instead of ending the humans as you could've, what did you Kings do? You sent the dragons away. As soon as I saw the dragon bridge, I knew I'd rather stay and fight for what was ours than leave."

"Do you honestly believe it was easy for us to watch our friends and family cross over the bridge? To know that we may never see them again?" Sebastian asked in disbelief.

Mikkel pointed a finger at Gianna. "As long as mortals roam this realm, the dragons willna be able to return!"

"We know."

"So you ran and hid on Dreagan," Mikkel said with a mirthless laugh as he dropped his arm. "You slept away centuries as the stories of dragons faded into myth and legend."

Sebastian gave a nod. "When we emerged, we were able to live among the morals."

"Why? What has that gotten you?" he demanded. "You only shift and fly at night or during storms. You hide everything there is about

Dreagan, from the dragons to the magic. You've forgotten what it is to be a Dragon King."

"What I have no' forgotten was my vow to protect the mortals."

Gold eyes full of hostility and repugnance looked him up and down. "Your first duty was to your clan and the dragons. Fuck the mortals."

"Your fight is with me," Sebastian said when he saw the way Mikkel was edging toward Gianna.

Mikkel laughed as he came even with her and lifted a lock of red hair in his hand. "Good luck getting to me."

With a roar, Sebastian launched himself at the Dark nearest him. His hand sunk into the Fae's chest and ripped out his heart before he spun to the next. He stumbled backward after being hit simultaneously with orbs of magic. The Dark magic burned through his clothes and skin into his cartilage, muscle, and bone. His body began to heal almost instantly, but nothing could save him from the agony.

As he fought a Dark, one came up behind him and kicked Sebastian in the back of the leg, sending him to his knee. More balls of magic pummeled him, briefly weakening him. The three Fae alternately hit him with their fists and magic. Sebastian let out a bellow as he dropped to his hands. He wanted to shift, he needed to shift. But there wasn't enough room.

He pushed himself up and got to his feet, gritting his teeth through the agony. He was more than capable of beating the Fae in human form, and he was going to do just that. When he spotted a Dark getting ready to throw another orb at him, Sebastian grabbed the Fae nearest him and used him as a shield.

The Dark screamed as the ball of magic landed on his chest, instantly sinking through his skin and withering the organs. The Fae flailed about before finally dying. Sebastian tossed aside the dead body as he gave a vicious uppercut to a Dark's chin, sending him flying backward.

He saw the other Fae start to teleport out and quickly grabbed his spinal column, jerking it out. Sebastian threw down what was left of the Fae and turned his gaze to Mikkel, who was watching the scene with interest.

With a glance in Gianna's direction, Sebastian walked to the Fae lying unconscious from his uppercut. He reached down and punched through the Dark's chest before yanking out his heart. Then he squeezed the still-beating organ until it burst.

Sebastian straightened, blood flowing down his arm before he flung the heart at Mikkel. "You only brought four Dark? Against a Dragon King?"

"I didn't bring just the Fae," Mikkel said.

Sebastian was done playing. "You've caused nothing but havoc for the last few years for us. That ends today. Right now."

"I don't think so," Mikkel said with a smile.

The only reason for someone to act so confidently was if they had an ace up their sleeve. One that had become a recent bane to the Dragon Kings. Sebastian could've kicked himself for forgetting about the Druid.

He shifted to the side when he heard the sound of heels clicking on the wood floor. His eyes turned toward the door he'd walked through earlier to find a tall woman clad in skintight black pants, a long-sleeved black turtleneck that molded to her body, and over-the-knee stiletto boots.

Her long black hair was slicked back into a high ponytail. She wore no jewelry except for silver finger rings that ended in long, sharp claws on her left hand. She halted, her feet spread as she gazed at him with greenish gold eyes.

"Dragon King," she said.

He noted her American accent, tinged with just a hint of Irish. "Druid."

So this was the woman who had enough Druid magic to alter the minds of two women from Dreagan?

Sebastian turned his head to Mikkel. "You speak of the dragons and our power. You talk of how we should've wiped the world of the mortals. Where is your power? Where is your desire to fight your own battles? You bring Dark Fae and now a Druid?"

"I'm saving myself for the important battles," Mikkel said with a cocky smile.

Sebastian gave a snort of laughter. "I doona believe that. You thought I was Ulrik. You had this set up before you knew it was me."

Mikkel shrugged and moved closer to Gianna. "Ulrik is a hindrance. I should've killed him when he was a youngling. Had I known he would become King of the Silvers, I would've."

"And who's to say you would've been King if there had been no

Ulrik? You've forgotten one crucial component to any dragon becoming Dragon King."

Mikkel cut him a harsh look. "I know it all too well. The dragon with the most magic and power gets to become King."

"It's no' just the magic and power. It's who the dragon is, their heart and soul. You've coveted what you couldna have. It has turned your heart black and your soul evil. You'd never become a Dragon King."

"It won't matter," Mikkel said. "I'm going to be King of Kings."

Sebastian looked at the Druid. "Did he promise you wouldna be harmed when he wipes out the mortals? Perhaps none of the Druids would? You do know it's a lie, aye? Regardless of the magic inside you, you're the verra thing he loathes—human. You'll be a reminder of the countless centuries he lost while waiting to rule it all."

"My business with him is no concern of yours," the Druid stated.

Sebastian lifted one shoulder in a shrug. He swung his head back to Mikkel to find Gianna staring at him as if she didn't know him, as if it were all some kind of macabre dream that she was eager to wake from.

"Shift," Mikkel demanded.

He'd known this was coming from the moment Mikkel began to tell Gianna their story. No doubt he'd threaten Gianna, leaving Sebastian no choice. The fact was, he wanted to shift, craved it as much as he hungered to have Gianna in his arms again. He looked into her green eyes as she stared at him with a frown beginning to form.

"You want to," Mikkel said. "I can see it on your face."

He wished the bastard would just shut up. Magic pulsed through Sebastian, throbbing in his palm, as he briefly thought of unleashing it upon Mikkel.

The only thing that stopped him was the knowledge that the Druid would go straight for Gianna. If Mikkel was anything like Ulrik—who was an amazing tactician—then he'd have thought of such events.

Sebastian looked to the Druid to find her standing with her arms crossed over her chest, a bored expression on her face. There was no fear or excitement. It was almost as if she'd seen dragons before. Mikkel, perhaps?

No, he didn't think Mikkel was able to shift, which meant he must not have all his magic unbound. Yet. It was most likely coming. Who had the Druid seen then? Ulrik? That didn't sound right either if Ulrik wasn't working with Mikkel. As much as Sebastian wanted to know, there wasn't time for him to go through each King to determine who she might've seen and when.

"Shift!" Mikkel yelled.

Sebastian had stalled long enough. He removed his boots and shirt before taking off his jeans. He stood there naked, his eyes locked with Gianna. She watched him with confusion, as if she couldn't wrap her head around what was happening.

Mikkel cackled loudly. "This is my favorite part. This is when the Dragon King gets to see a true reaction. Do you fear it, Sebastian?"

More than he cared to admit, but he wouldn't let Mikkel, Gianna, or the Druid know that. As Sebastian looked at Gianna, he wished he'd told her something about himself. He'd held back, not because he thought she might scoff at him, but because he feared she might accept him.

If she had, he wouldn't have been able to leave her. The truth settled in his stomach like a rock. He'd told himself he was protecting her, when in fact he'd been guarding his own heart. Because...he loved her.

He took a deep breath. When he shifted, he'd have one shot. As much as he wanted Mikkel, he was going after the Druid. Without her, Mikkel would be exposed and easily hunted. The Druid was the one more capable of damage than Mikkel, so she was the one who would die first.

With a plan in place, Sebastian shifted. It felt glorious to be in his true form, though he wasn't able to lift his head as he wanted. A growl rumbled in his chest. If he unfurled his wings, he'd crush the crates around him.

In all of this, he hadn't taken his gaze off Gianna. Her eyes widened in disbelief when he shifted. She blinked several times, as if trying to take it all in. But she didn't scream or run away.

Then she stood and took a step toward him.

Chapter Eighteen

This couldn't possibly be real.

And yet it was.

In big, bold Technicolor.

Gianna couldn't pull her eyes away from the dragon—from Sebastian. Her breath was coming in great gasps as she looked at him in awe, as well as a dose of panic at something so huge.

Glistening metallic scales the color of gunmetal blue met her gaze. His wide alabaster eyes watched her. There was a thread of panic running through her, but during the time she'd spent with Sebastian, he hadn't hurt her once. And somehow she knew he wouldn't now either.

Slowly that panic and fear began to dissipate, and she was able to look at him with a calm mind. She took another halting step toward him. He was so massive she had to crane her neck back to see him. She let her gaze run over him, noting how the color of his scales darkened on random patches of his body. All four limbs had six digits on each foot with extremely long claws. His wings were tucked against him, and she had the crazy urge to ask him to spread them so she could see them in all their glory.

At the back of his skull was a bony plate that projected backward to protect his neck, while a single horn protruded from the base of his chin. A row of spines ran from the base of his skull down his back to the tip of his tail where there was a bladelike extension on the end.

She wanted to touch him, to feel his scales beneath her palms. The need for that connection drove her, propelling her to take another step and another toward the beast and away from Mikkel—who, curiously, didn't stop her.

The moment she made contact with Sebastian, something zapped from his scales into her hand. She jerked her gaze upward to his dragon eyes. That's when she realized the safest place for her was standing next to the giant dragon.

The Dragon King.

Sebastian shifted so that she stood between his two front legs. She barely had time to get used to that when, without warning, he opened his mouth and fire came billowing out, right toward the woman he kept calling Druid.

His rumble of a roar filled the area. The next instant, Sebastian was in human form once more. He roughly shoved her behind him. Then he blew out a breath toward Mikkel, except it wasn't air that came out, but lightning.

Gianna glanced over at the fire containing the Druid. Her mouth fell open when the woman held her hands up, waving them about with her lips moving, while somehow extinguishing the fire.

So...Druid really meant...Druid. After Gianna witnessed Sebastian's fight with the Dark Fae, the Druid didn't come as such a shock. Other than the fact she wished she had her own magic right now. With Sebastian containing Mikkel, Gianna decided to try another tactic.

She stalked to the Druid and stood before her once the fire was out. "Leave," Gianna demanded.

The Druid raised a black brow as her greenish gold eyes watched her. "I like your courage, but I can't do that."

"Sure you can. You turn around and walk away while you still can."

"You think your Dragon King will kill me?" There was a hint of a smile on the Druid's lips. "It will come, but not by his hands."

Gianna heard Mikkel yell in pain. She opened her mouth to speak again, but the Druid waved her hand from right to left, and Gianna went flying.

Her back slammed into the corner of a crate, knocking the breath from her. She gasped for air, her hand over her ribs as the pain sliced through her. Even as she worked through the blinding agony, her eyes tracked the Druid, who was making her way toward Sebastian.

Gianna wanted to call out to Sebastian, to warn him. But there was no need as he turned and spotted the Druid. His eyes narrowed into dangerous slits as he let loose another volley of lightning directed right at the woman.

As soon as the bolts slammed into and around her, the Druid let out a cry of pain. Her body was frozen as it jerked helplessly from the currents. After another few seconds, Sebastian held up his hand. Though Gianna didn't see anything come from his palm, it was obviously magic that tossed the Druid out the door before it slammed shut.

Sometime during all of that, Gianna was able to take a normal breath. She dragged air into her greedy lungs as the stinging began to diminish enough that she could push herself up on one hand to look for Mikkel.

She found him on the ground unmoving. Was it over then? Or nearly? She truly hoped so, because she'd just about reached her limit of...well, everything.

Sebastian turned to her, his gaze darting to the closed door where the Druid had been flung.

"I'm fine," Gianna said. "Go do what you need."

"Stay here. I'll return." Then he was striding to the door, yanking it open, and disappearing.

Gianna had no doubt Sebastian would take care of the Druid, and quite frankly, she didn't care how he did it. Not after everything she'd seen and heard. Whoever the Druid was, she had chosen to work with Mikkel, and that made her a threat in Gianna's book.

She sat up and took stock of her body while keeping an eye on Mikkel. He might be unconscious, but she didn't think they'd get lucky enough that he was dead. She winced when she took a breath. There were various aches and twinges, but it was nothing to the burns on Sebastian's body that he sustained during the Dark attack. Burns that she had seen begin to heal.

A Dragon King. And immortal.

Why wasn't she more shocked at it all?

It certainly wasn't because of the story Mikkel told. The tale might have helped explain things, but there had always been something uncommon about Sebastian that went far beyond his confidence and charming smile.

Now she knew. He had magic. No. That wasn't it at all. The reason was because he was a dragon.

There was a smile on her face when she leaned her head back

against a crate and closed her eyes. Her lover was a Dragon King. And she couldn't wait to be in his arms again.

As her breathing evened out, she thought about Mikkel. For years, she'd worked for a maniac without even knowing it. She'd known that not all of his business contacts were on the up and up, but she hadn't delved deeper.

That was because she'd known what she might find, and she hadn't cared. That apathy was not the woman she knew herself to be. It was a part of her life that she would close the door on and move forward, but never forget.

It would always be there, a constant reminder of how she let indifference control her. The complete and total disregard to what was moral and what wasn't. The new her wanted to slam her fist into Mikkel's face.

She lifted her head, her eyes opening as she contemplated doing just that. When she thought of how he'd roughly handled her, how he'd cut her finger and yanked her hair, she wanted to hurt him. Mikkel would continue to harm others.

Gianna held her ribs before she tucked her legs under her and climbed to her feet. She put her hands on the crate. Then she quietly walked to where Mikkel was lying.

Only when she made it around the crates, he was gone. She hastily looked about, thinking he might have crawled somewhere. Then she began to search behind the numerous crates, but she quickly discovered that he was well and truly gone.

The sound of footsteps had her spinning toward the door. When she saw Sebastian, relief filled her. His frown, however, spoke volumes about his anger.

"She's gone. The damn Druid is gone," he grumbled.

She wrinkled her nose. "Then I really hate to tell you that Mikkel is, too."

Sebastian said nothing as he hurriedly searched the room for Mikkel. All the while she looked over his fine body. The wounds were almost healed, attesting to his immortality. Then she looked at his dragon tattoo.

Was it merely a stroke of chance that she had gotten a dragon tat? Or had it been something more like the hand of Fate reaching down and turning her in the direction she was supposed to go?

"I had them both," Sebastian said, annoyance deepening his voice. She shivered against the cold. "What now?"

"I should look for them." Then his gaze landed on her. "After I get you home and make sure you're safe."

"What about this whole Dragon King thing?"

He searched her gaze but didn't come closer. "Knowledge of us usually puts people in danger."

"And you were trying to save me from that," she finished. "I understand. I'd have done the same thing. But I know now. I saw."

"So you did. You didna run. Why?"

"I gather from that statement that others normally run away?"

He gave a single nod.

She licked her lips and walked to him. If he wouldn't come to her, she would go to him. She stopped before him and stuffed her hands in her pockets so she wouldn't reach out for him, even though she craved to touch him.

"I told you about my marriage," she said. "After the divorce, the thought of another man in my life gave me hives. I put my effort into my career. It wasn't until I saw you at the bar that I found I wanted to be with you. When I was, I forgot about my past and only saw the present and how wonderful it was to be with you. Even had I wanted to ignore the attraction, I couldn't have. It was entirely too strong."

She stopped and swallowed, hoping Sebastian would say something, but he continued to look at her. "And I realize I was part of your plan to get to Mikkel. You're leaving Venice, but before you do, I have something I need to say. Our time together was short, but you cleared away the fog I was living in. You helped me to remember who I used to be and the dreams I once had.

"I knew when I met up with you the other morning that I was putting my heart in jeopardy. And I didn't care. I wanted to feel again. So it was no surprise when I left your palazzo that I realized I'd fallen in lo—"

She never got to finish her sentence. Sebastian grabbed her face and yanked her against him, kissing her deeply. She sank against him, her arms wrapping around his neck as she forgot about her aches and pains. His warmth enveloped her as his kiss made her toes curl. They could've kissed for eternity and she wouldn't have cared. She was in his arms, the only place she wanted to be.

He finally ended it and pressed his forehead against hers. "I came to seduce you, but you're the one who stole my heart. Completely. Utterly. I was willing to walk away to keep you out of our war, but it was more difficult than I ever counted on."

"Does that mean...you love me?"

"Aye, I love you," he whispered huskily and kissed her again.

Her heart was bursting with happiness when the kiss ended and she rested her cheek against his chest to hold him tightly. "What now?"

"We get out of Venice."

"To where?"

"Dreagan," he answered.

She leaned back to look at him. "Like the Scotch?"

"Aye. We distill it."

Her eyes widened at the news. "Now I understand where the money comes from. But tell me something else."

"Anything."

"Is the story Mikkel told me true?"

The light faded from Sebastian's eyes a little. "Sadly, it is."

"That's why Ulrik was banished, and why you're looking for him."

"He walked alone for centuries. I should've been there for him."

"You were today," she said. "How is it you don't hate humans? And why was any mention of dragons erased from history?"

His topaz eyes crinkled at the corners. "We made sure there was never any history of us. As for the other, no' all mortals are bad, just as no' all dragons are like Mikkel."

"But you sent the dragons away."

He wound a lock of her hair around his finger. "Aye. We miss them terribly, but mortals and dragons can no' live in the same realm."

"That makes me sad."

"The past is the past. It can no' be changed. But the future is as yet unwritten. With your help, I learned all I needed from Mikkel to let the other Kings know our target isna Ulrik but his uncle."

Gianna looked to where Mikkel had fallen. "Who can apparently disappear."

"The Druid as well. Right now she's a bigger threat. I'd intended to kill her."

"She said you weren't the Dragon King who would end her life."

Sebastian's forehead crinkled in a frown at that news. "It helps to know that a King will end her life."

"But will it be soon enough?"

"It better be. She's done enough damage already," he said as he pulled away and began to dress.

Gianna took his hand once he finished and they walked to the door. They exchanged looks, his fingers tightening on hers.

"It's going to be all right," he promised.

To her surprise, she truly believed it would.

Chapter Nineteen

"I'm going to kill him!"

Eilish watched Mikkel from her position in one of the chairs as he paced the office inside his palazzo.

"What the hell did you think bringing me back here?" he demanded as he whirled around to face her. "Here? The verra place they'll start looking for me!"

It was on the tip of her tongue to tell him to "fek off," but she kept the comment to herself. Mikkel might be a master at setting the stage for his coup, but he had yet to learn to control his rage, which always bled through in his Scots brogue.

She merely stared at him, refusing to speak until he calmed. He huffed loudly before he began pacing again. Eilish took that time to mentally check her body. There were going to be many bruises, and she was fairly certain at least one rib was cracked along with her broken wrist, thanks to the lightning strike.

While Mikkel grumbled to himself, she closed her eyes and let her magic begin to heal her body. As the magic moved through her like a comforting hand, the pain diminished. When the last of it vanished, she opened her eyes to find that Mikkel stood before her. His gold eyes were narrowed, anger contorting his features.

He and Ulrik looked so much alike they could pass for twins, but that's where their similarities ended. Ulrik's patience startled even her. Not that he didn't get angry. She'd seen a flash of it in his eyes recently when he'd visited her at her pub, but he hadn't let it control him. Not like Mikkel.

It was her first time meeting Ulrik, and she'd realized right away why Mikkel hated his nephew. He was everything Mikkel wanted to be—and wasn't. Ulrik was everything Mikkel believed he deserved—and didn't.

She was really going to hate killing Ulrik.

"You're welcome for saving your ass and keeping you out of the hands of the Dragon Kings," she said as she stood and strode past Mikkel to the doorway.

"You can't walk away from me."

She rolled her eyes at his dramatics, but didn't look his way. "Watch me."

"I own you!"

That brought her to a halt. Rage stormed inside her with a ferocity that she contemplated unleashing on Mikkel. Slowly, she turned to face him. Magic crackled through her veins, making her skin tingle while urging her to wreak her brand of havoc on him.

She almost gave in. It was such a tempting thought that she was raising her hand when she recalled their agreement. "Let's get something straight right now. You don't own me. And you never will. I agreed to help you in exchange for information."

"Information you won't be able to obtain by anyone else. Only me," Mikkel stated brusquely.

The one thing she'd always promised herself was that she would never be beholden to anyone again—and look what she'd gotten herself into. It was the information Mikkel dangled before her, teasing her with, that kept her answering his summons and demands, but she was growing weary of it all.

"I can tell you who your real mother is," Mikkel said.

They'd been through this multiple times. She knew the outcome, and yet she found herself saying, "Tell me."

"Not yet."

"I'm beginning to think you don't really know."

Mikkel's smile was slow as it pulled at his lips. "Is that a chance you're willing to take? After searching for so long?"

Man, she really hated him. One day, the two of them would clash, and she wasn't going to come out the loser.

"You should go," she said. "Sebastian will be coming for you soon."

"There's one thing you need to do first."

Eilish could well imagine what he wanted of her, but still she asked, "What?"

"Wipe Sebastian's mind of everything I told him. I don't want him to recall any of it or me."

She crossed her arms over her chest, surprised by his request. "All right."

"Kill Gianna. Make Sebastian believe he did it."

Now this was the Mikkel she knew and loathed. "I'll see it done."

She didn't wait around for him to leave before she touched one of the silver finger rings and disappeared.

* * * *

Con broke the surface of the water beneath the palazzo Dreagan owned and climbed up the dock. He ran upstairs, unmindful of the trail of water he left in his wake, all the while calling Sebastian's name through the mental link. The longer it went on without a response, the more worried he became.

He used his magic to open the door of the palazzo. After drying off and finding clothes, he was soon on the streets of Venice headed to the location that Ryder sent him by the mental link.

No matter how many times Con called Sebastian's name through their link, it was only silence that greeted him. There were no sounds of roars from a dragon, so Con held out hope that Sebastian hadn't shifted. Especially since Ulrik had no compunction about doing the same, as he'd shown everyone in Paris when he'd attacked Asher.

The closer Con got to the building, the more alert he became. He expected Dark to jump out or to see some sign of Ulrik. But there was nothing.

Not even a sound.

He found the entrance of the building and easily got through the lock with a little magic. When he stepped through and looked around, he saw evidence of a battle. There were scorch marks from dragon fire, but they had been quickly extinguished. There were also marks from Sebastian's lightning. Unease curled through him. His gaze lifted to the cracked crates. Then he saw the blood.

He knelt beside one of the puddles and drew in a deep breath.

"Dark Fae," he mumbled.

At least it wasn't Sebastian's. Or the mortal female's. But where were the two of them? And where was Mikkel or Ulrik?

Con spotted the splintered wood near another door and walked to it. Rubbing his finger over it, he looked beyond into the corridor to see a wall that someone had impacted hard. Beyond it was a tunnel. He followed the pathway, spotting more Dark Fae blood as well as human blood. The few drops meant the mortal wasn't seriously injured. Most likely it was used as a means to lure Sebastian.

Con didn't stop until he reached the open door into the palazzo. He stood at the doorway and listened for any sounds of another somewhere inside. The structure was completely empty, shocking him.

He walked to the office window and looked out to see that he wasn't far from Dreagan's palazzo. Whether this was Mikkel's or Ulrik's home, they were entirely too close for his comfort. It made him realize it was time to have a look at their other properties and their neighbors.

Con tried once more to call out to Sebastian. When there was nothing, he then said, *"Ryder. Bast isna here. Has he contacted you?"*

"No' a peep," Ryder replied.

Con turned and looked back through the tunnel he'd walked as well as the hidden doorway. *"Me either, and I've been trying to get him since I reached Venice. Something is amiss."*

"You think it's the Druid?"

"It's a possibility. There were signs of a battle at the building, and I counted at least six Dark that were taken out."

"Way to go, Bast. I'm doing a facial search of Venice near the building that I sent you to in ord— I got them! Bast and Gianna are headed to our palazzo."

"Keep him there, and find out why he's no' answering me. I'm going to go looking for Ulrik or Mikkel. Or both."

"You really shouldna do that alone."

Con cut off the link before Ryder could say more. Before Con left the palazzo, he walked the entire residence and searched each room. There was nothing personal in the house other than clothes, which didn't tell him who lived there. There was a nagging feeling that kept pushing him to find Sebastian, but Con didn't want to lose this opportunity to take out Ulrik or Mikkel.

The fact there were two of them irked him. At least he thought there were two. He had yet to hear from Sebastian, but it was better to err on the side of caution after everything that had been happening.

Disappointed in not finding anything to link Ulrik to the palazzo, Con left and began to search the streets for Ulrik—or anyone looking like him. He'd been putting off the inevitable with his old friend, but it was time things came to a head.

He was tired of waiting for Ulrik to make a move, tired of hoping that something, anything might go right for him and the Kings in their war, but that's not what a King did. Of all people, Con should know that.

He'd stayed his hand once with Ulrik, and it had led them to this moment. Once and for all he was putting sentiment aside and doing what had to be done.

No matter the consequences.

* * * *

Eilish was still battling the effects of the bolts of electricity Sebastian had thrown her way. She hadn't prepared for that, and that was her fault. It was a mistake she wouldn't make again with him or any of the other Dragon Kings.

She took a deep breath and settled into the corner of the bedroom amid the shadows as she waited for Sebastian and Gianna to return. The pair fascinated her. Even after everything Gianna had learned about her lover, she still looked at Sebastian as if he were her very world.

Mikkel had been sure Gianna would attempt to run away. What was it that kept Gianna still? What was it that made her walk to Sebastian in dragon form and touch his scales? What was it that made Gianna trust him so implicitly?

As if her thoughts had conjured them, the couple came into the room holding hands. Gianna was smiling as Sebastian told her this was the best place for them to rest. Gianna kicked off her shoes and shrugged out of her ruined coat before taking the pins from her fallen hair. All the while, Sebastian watched her as if he would die if he didn't.

Eilish almost felt sorry for them. They had no idea what was about to happen. She drew in a breath. His dragon magic had been difficult to get through, but she had managed it. Though it cost her greatly, leaving her drained and lethargic.

Perhaps that was why she remained in the corner observing them for so long instead of doing what she was sent to do. She was taken aback at the way Sebastian caressed Gianna's red hair as if he were mesmerized by it. And the way Gianna leaned toward him.

But it was the look in the Dragon King's eyes—a look that was undeniably love, which made her heart catch. That kind of deep emotion alarmed her. She couldn't imagine ever caring for anyone or anything to such a degree that they would have power over her.

"How long until we go to Dreagan?" Gianna asked.

Sebastian shrugged and jerked out of his shirt. "A few hours. I want to look for Mikkel in the meantime."

"You won't find him," Eilish said as she pushed away from the corner, dropping the magic that had hidden her.

Sebastian whirled toward her, his eyes narrowing in anger. "How the fuck are you here?"

"Magic," she said and held up her hand, waving her silver-clad fingers.

"That's no' possible."

She wrinkled her nose. "I'll admit, dragon magic is tough, but I got through it."

"I intended to kill you back there," Sebastian said.

He had no idea how close he'd come, and she wasn't going to tell him. If she hadn't used her magic at the last second, she might very well be dead. "Perhaps you can try another time."

"What do you want?" Gianna said. "We've done nothing to you."

"That doesn't matter in war." Eilish shrugged as she returned her gaze to the Dragon King. "You're fighting a battle you can't win."

Sebastian gave a loud snort. "Against a Druid? Aye, I can win."

"Really? You're a Dragon King, a being who could rule everyone, yet you continue to hide."

"You think you know me," he stated with a sneer.

She knew much more than she ever wanted to. "If you shift, you'd have the upper hand with me, but you won't do it. Mainly because you don't want to chance humans seeing you or destroying this gorgeous palazzo and drawing attention to yourself. You won't use magic, because you feel as if you can best me without it. Both are mistakes you'll live to regret."

"Thanks for the warning," he said and opened his mouth, blowing out a breath.

Eilish raised a shield of magic, but she was still weak from before and it did nothing. She bit back a yelp as the lightning hit her again and again. When she fell to her hands and knees, Sebastian halted his attack. It was the very thing he shouldn't have done.

"A mistake," she said through gasping breaths. Then she lifted her hand, magic shooting from her palm and slamming into Sebastian. Her magic knocked him unconscious. She quickly did the same with Gianna.

She dropped her head, letting it hang as she battled the pain ripping through her. That damn lightning was vicious, and it would be too soon if she never felt it again. For long minutes she remained in that position, letting her breathing even out.

When she finally lifted her head, she looked to Sebastian. It took a great amount of effort to crawl to him. It was a slow process, and one she knew would be the death of her if she didn't prepare better before she killed both Ulrik and Con. Then Mikkel.

Once she was beside Sebastian, she looked down at the Dragon King. Her hand was drawn to the dragon tat on his abdomen. She'd seen how the tattoo wrapped around his leg and ended at his foot. There had been a surge of relief that it wasn't the tattoo she saw in her dreams—the same surge that went through her now.

Her body wanted to shut down and regain its strength, but she fought to remain awake. She put her hand on Sebastian's forehead. Then she pushed magic into his mind, the spell worded so that anything to do with Mikkel in Venice would be wiped.

As she was finished, a drop of blood landed on the back of her hand. She gazed at it in frustration and anxiety. She needed to finish and soon. She wiped at her nose and turned to Gianna.

Despite what Mikkel demanded, she couldn't—and wouldn't—kill Gianna. It was an action she might come to regret, but she wasn't Mikkel's assassin.

But there could be others.

Eilish said a quick protection spell over Gianna after also wiping away memories of Mikkel. Then she touched the finger rings together to take her back to Ireland and her sanctuary.

Chapter Twenty

Gianna woke slowly, as if she were clawing her way through thick mist that seemed to continue to tug her back down again and again. She fought through it when a feeling of dread consumed her, something urging her to rouse. She became frantic as she tried repeatedly to wake, not knowing what was pushing her.

It wasn't until she finally managed to pry open her eyes that she saw the beamed ceiling. As soon as she did, the previous events slammed into her. She gasped, her heart pounding as she thought of Sebastian. She rolled over and sat up, her gaze locking on him.

"Sebastian." It was meant to be a scream, but it came out as a hoarse whisper as she put her hand on him.

"He willna wake."

The sound of the male voice startled her. Gianna jerked her head in the direction of the words and found herself staring into eyes as black as midnight. The man was sitting with his forearms on his knees in a chair on the opposite side of the room.

"I couldna get you to wake either," he said as he ran a hand through his short, wavy blond hair and leaned back.

She kept her hand on Sebastian's neck, the feel of his pulse beneath her fingers allowing the band about her heart to ease. "Who are you?"

"Constantine."

So this was Con. She looked down at Sebastian. "She said she was going to erase all of his memories."

"She who?" Con asked.

"The Druid."

The sound of his footsteps approached as he walked to her. "Memories of who?"

Gianna opened her mouth to answer as she looked up at him, but the words wouldn't come. "I...I can't remember."

"Did you meet Mikkel?"

"Mikkel? Who's that?"

Con muttered something beneath his breath as he turned his head away. He looked back at her. "Forget it. What were Bast's plans?"

"We were going to Dreagan."

The answer had come quickly, as if she knew it without question. How could she be so certain of that, but not know what memories the Druid wanted to take away? And how did she remember the Druid?

"Doona think too hard," Con warned. "The more you try to remember, the more those memories will drift further back in your mind."

She smoothed Sebastian's golden brown hair away from his face and attempted to take Con's advice. "How is it I'm awake and he isn't? He's a Dragon King."

Con let out a loud, resigned sigh. "So you do know of us."

"Yes."

He gave a nod and said, "Rhi."

"Is someone else with you?" Gianna asked, looking around. "Someone who could help with Sebastian?"

"I'm here alone, but I've called to someone. There's nothing wrong with Bast physically. It's his mind."

Gianna said, "He has lightning in his breath. Do you have some power that can fix him?"

"I can heal anything, but his mind isna damaged. He'd heal himself otherwise."

Right. Because she'd seen him heal after... Once more her memories just stopped. She rubbed her eyes. When she next looked at Con, there was a woman of indescribable beauty with black hair and silver eyes standing next to him.

The woman was clad in a white chiffon shirt that tucked into black leather pants. It was the strappy black Christian Louboutin heels that caught Gianna's eye.

"Nice shoes," she said before she could stop herself.

The woman looked down at her feet and smiled. "Thanks. You like shoes?"

There was a brief hesitation as Gianna heard the Irish accent. It made her think of the Dark Fae. "Love them."

"Then we should go shopping sometime."

Gianna returned her smile. It had been a very long time since she'd had such a friend, and she was more than ready to retake that part of her life. "I'd like that."

"Really?" Con asked in disbelief as he looked at the woman. He held out his hand toward Sebastian and said, "Can you no' see we have a wee problem? It's why I called you here."

The woman raised a brow as she glared at him. "Of course I can see your 'wee problem.' I'm not blind. And it's not like Sebastian can go anywhere. Besides, you aren't freaking out."

"I'm Gianna," she said, holding her hand out to the woman. "Can you help us?"

The woman came down on her haunches on the other side of Sebastian and shook Gianna's hand. "I'm Rhi."

"Light Fae?"

Rhi nodded slowly as she glanced at Sebastian. "I am. What happened?"

"The Druid," Con said.

With two words, Rhi's entire attitude changed. Gone was the almost whimsical attitude. In its place was a warrior who was ready to run headfirst into battle. Rhi peered at Gianna intently. "Did she do anything to you?"

Before Gianna could answer, Con said, "When I arrived, both were unconscious. I waited over thirty minutes before Gianna woke. I can no' get Bast to respond."

"The Druid took his memories," Gianna explained.

Rhi and Con exchanged a look.

"How do you know?" Con asked.

Gianna opened her mouth to reply but there was no explanation. "I don't know why I remember that and nothing else."

Rhi stood. "Did Sebastian have a run-in with Ulrik and the Druid?"

"Sebastian came to find Mikkel," Con explained.

Gianna wished she knew who Mikkel was. She had a feeling she was supposed to, but like Con said, every time she tried to force the memories, they retreated further away. She put her hand to her head and rubbed her temple as pain formed. If only she could put a face to the Druid or figure out something, anything instead of feeling so damn helpless.

Rhi held out a hand to her and Gianna took it, allowing herself to be pulled to her feet. She swayed, the room spinning. It was Rhi who steadied her.

"Easy," Rhi said.

Con frowned as he stared at Gianna. "She just woke."

"Then there's a chance Sebastian will soon as well," Rhi replied.

Gianna pulled her gaze from Sebastian and looked at the two of them. "He was adamant we leave and return to Dreagan."

Rhi rubbed her hand up and down Gianna's back. "We will very soon. So you know all about the Dragon Kings and Fae?"

"And Ulrik," she said.

It was the moan coming from Sebastian that silenced them. Gianna pulled away from Rhi and dropped to her knees beside him. "Sebastian? Can you hear me?"

His hand moved and found hers, his fingers gripping her tightly.

She looked at their hands before raising her gaze to his face. "I'm here. Everything is all right, but you need to wake up. Now."

"Gianna," he whispered as his eyes opened and locked with hers.

She smiled, her heart nearly bursting in her chest. "You scared me."

"You're no' hurt?" he asked as his other hand rose up and brushed her cheek.

"She's fine," Con said.

Sebastian lowered his arm and turned his head to find Rhi and Con. Gianna watched the three of them stare at each other before Sebastian sat up and raked a hand through his long hair. He grunted, squeezing his eyes shut. "What happened?"

"Do you remember a Druid?" Rhi asked.

Sebastian nodded and opened his eyes. "She was here. Standing right where you are. I thought she was going to kill Gianna."

"Did you fight her?" Con asked.

Gianna remembered and hurried to say, "He did. With his lightning."

"And she still bested you?" Rhi asked with a worried frown.

Con crossed his arms over his chest. "How did she get inside the palazzo?"

"Her magic," Sebastian said as he climbed to his feet.

Gianna stood beside him, their hands still linked. "What about Mikkel?"

Sebastian gave her an odd look. "Who's that?"

She turned her head to Con and shrugged. "The Druid said she was going to take his memories. Whoever this Mikkel is, maybe that's what she took."

"Apparently she took yours as well," Con said.

Rhi moved her hair over her shoulder. "Looks like we need to find Ulrik. Perhaps he can shed some light on this."

"I agree," Con said. "Can you take those two to Dreagan and meet me back here?"

Rhi was reaching for them. Gianna didn't know what was happening, but Sebastian seemed fine with it, so she didn't say anything. Right before Rhi grabbed them, she stilled, her face going white. Con and Sebastian jerked as if struck in the stomach.

"Rhi?" Con asked as he grasped her arm.

The Fae turned her wide, silver gaze to him. "You felt that, didn't you?"

"I didn't," Gianna said. "What happened?"

Sebastian tightened his grip on her hand. "Magic. We felt something powerful move through the realm."

Gianna wasn't sure she'd ever get used to Earth being called a realm. "I can guess by your faces that it isn't good."

"No," Rhi said as she put a hand to her stomach.

Con didn't release his hold of Rhi. "It was Fae."

The Fae nodded slowly. "I need to see what happened."

Gianna wasn't prepared to blink and find herself standing in another room. In the next instant, Rhi was gone. Gianna looked at Sebastian and Con, both had worried looks on their faces.

"Usaeil?" Sebastian asked.

Con shrugged and stalked off. Gianna watched him go, trying to figure out where she belonged in this world of magic, dragons, and Fae.

"Welcome to Dreagan," Sebastian said.

She blinked and looked at him in surprise. "Truly?"

"The Fae can teleport."

"But not the Dragon Kings?" she teased.

He gave her a teasing look. "We're dragons. We can shift. We've never had a need to teleport."

She licked her lips as all humor left her. "I feel like I'm forgetting something really important. Like it's life and death."

"Me as well." He frowned and gave a shake of his head. "But I can no' figure out what it is."

"Will we ever remember?"

He brought her hand to his lips. "I can no' say."

"What happened with Rhi just a moment ago?"

His topaz eyes clouded with concern. "I doona know, but I'm sure we will soon."

When he turned and tugged her after him, she gladly walked by his side through the manor. It was a mix of classic and contemporary, dark and light. The many windows allowed light to pour into the house, and the various rugs added layers of texture.

It wasn't hard to miss the dragons. Some were obvious, some more difficult to find, but they were everywhere. It was as they turned to walk up the stairs that she got her first look outside.

The mountains and glens were covered in snow. She spotted cattle and sheep and the hint of a red roof in the distance. She couldn't wait to explore all of it. It wasn't just the idea of being in another country. This was Sebastian's home, and she wanted to know every inch, what he loved, and where his favorite places were.

They reached the second floor and walked down the long corridor of rooms until Sebastian stopped at one and opened the door. She walked inside and smiled when her gaze landed on the bed and the gunmetal blue comforter.

"The others are going to have questions for us," he said as he led her to a chair before the fireplace.

The crackle of the fire and its warmth was just what she needed. She sat, releasing his hand so he could do the same. "I know."

"I had a mission when I went to Venice."

"Was it Mikkel?" she asked. "Con kept asking me about him."

Sebastian shrugged, a helpless look coming over his face. "I have this feeling that I found what I was looking for, but I doona know what that is."

"Then maybe we aren't supposed to know."

His gaze met hers. "Maybe no', but I want to find the Druid who did this to us."

"I do as well. She took something from us both."

He pushed out of the chair and knelt before her, taking her hands. "But she didna take you from me. Because she didna kill you, I'll let her live."

"You're right. She could've easily taken my life. Why didn't she?"

"I doona know nor care right now. I have you, and we're back at Dreagan. To me, that's a win."

She wrapped her arms around him, holding him close as she squeezed her eyes shut. "I get the feeling that this came close to not happening."

"It doesna matter now," he soothed in his sexy voice.

"But it does." As much as she didn't want to think about the future, she had to. They'd professed their love for each other—that she remembered vividly, just as she did every aspect of her time with Sebastian—but she wasn't going to take for granted that she would remain at Dreagan.

He pulled back and cupped one of her cheeks as he grinned at her. "Ach, lass. Did you no' realize that when I told you that I loved you that I meant I wanted you to be mine? Forever."

"I..." She really didn't know what to say. "Because mates become immortal with Dragon Kings."

Sebastian's forehead creased. "I doona remember telling you our story."

"Because you didn't. Though I can't recall who did," she said.

"It doesna matter, and aye, you'd become immortal."

"I want to be with you, but I need some time to get used to all of this."

There was also the little fact that she'd resigned from her position. Nothing was holding her in Venice. It didn't bother her that she didn't know what she was going to do as far as a job went, because she loved Sebastian. Whatever she decided to choose would be something she wanted to do, and be happy doing it.

Sebastian had taught her that.

He stroked a hand down her face. "Of course. And if you never want to perform the ceremony, we willna. As long as you're by my side is enough."

She smiled in response, even though she knew it wouldn't be enough. She'd continue to age and eventually die. There was no telling how many others Sebastian had watched die or what it might do mentally and emotionally to an immortal. Yet, he put no pressure on her. And for that she would be eternally grateful.

"Stay here with me on Dreagan," he said. "Let me love you, and love me in return. I'll share my life with you for as long as you'll have me, because the alternative isna something I want to even consider."

She couldn't believe this amazing Dragon King was really hers. "I'll love you fiercely, my beautiful dragon. And I expect nothing less from you."

"You have my word," he vowed.

She leaned forward, sealing their promise with a kiss.

Then he pulled her down on the floor before the fire and held her close. There were no words to describe what happened in Venice, but both knew it was significant. Nor did she doubt that Sebastian would find the Druid who had done this to them and get their memories back.

But all of that seemed a world away now that she was on Dreagan, reclining in the arms of her lover.

The dragon who made her *burn*.

Epilogue

Perth, Scotland

Ulrik wasn't sure why he'd come back to The Silver Dragon. His antique shop was closed until further notice since Mikkel and Eilish had intruded. Mikkel had sent the Druid to kill him, but Ulrik wasn't going to go down that easily.

He stood down the street from his shop. He'd lived above it for several decades, but it wasn't his home. His home had been Dreagan—a place he'd been banished from. Though that didn't stop him from sneaking in and visiting his Silvers.

Movement out of the corner of his eye stopped him as he was turning away. He looked back and watched as a black Range Rover pulled up alongside the curb in front of the store. The vehicle door opened, and a tall man stepped out of the driver's side.

Ulrik was so dumbfounded that he stood frozen as he watched Sebastian walk to the entrance of the store. His gaze narrowed while he observed Bast test the door to see if it was unlocked before hanging something on the handle. Sebastian didn't linger. He got back in the SUV and drove off.

Ulrik waited ten minutes before he made his way to the storefront. His steps slowed, then stopped as he reached the door and saw the thin strip of leather. On it was the ring he'd given Sebastian so long ago.

He grasped the band, unhooking the leather. He stuffed it in his pocket and touched the silver bracelet to teleport away.

For the first time, he didn't feel alone. Sebastian wanted Ulrik to know that he was on his side by leaving the ring. Ulrik wasn't going to let this opportunity slip away.

* * * *

Light Fae Castle, Ireland

Rhi stood on the windswept cliffs looking out at the sea. She knew only magic of significant power could go through the realm like a shockwave. And she knew who was to blame—Usaeil.

It had taken seconds within the walls of the Light Castle to know that the queen wasn't there. The Light had been agitated by the rumors of the Reapers return, but they were downright hysterical now.

Off in the distance was Rhi's watcher—a Reaper who was never far. Ever since she'd gained back the memories that had been taken from her by Death, her Reaper had kept his distance. Partly because of the magic she'd used to keep him from following her. Yet Daire always managed to find her.

She wanted to ask him what he thought Usaeil was doing, but she knew he wouldn't answer. In all the time he had followed her, not once had he spoken. It wasn't until she joined in the Reapers fight with someone named Bran that Daire spoke to her and she'd finally seen him.

It was the uncertainty that kept her there looking out over the vast blue sea. Did she try to lead the Light? If she did, Usaeil would see it as an attempt to take the throne, and there would be a battle. That's not what the Light Fae needed.

But neither could Rhi no longer act. Their people needed someone to lead them, to guide them. Usaeil was backing her into a corner, and lessening her options with every day. If only the queen would take her rightful place in the castle instead of parading around the world as some famous American actress.

Soon, Rhi and Con would confront Usaeil about the picture she'd taken of Con and sold to the human tabloids in an effort to force the King of Dragon King's hand to take her as his mate. It was during this clash that Rhi would give the queen an ultimatum—return to the Light Castle or else.

Because there was something dark and treacherous on the horizon, and it was coming straight for Rhi. And she didn't intend to go down without a fight.

* * * *

Also from 1001 Dark Nights and Donna Grant, discover Dragon King and Dragon Fever.

Sign up for the 1001 Dark Nights Newsletter
and be entered to win a Tiffany Key necklace.

There's a contest every month!

Go to www.1001DarkNights.com to subscribe.

As a bonus, all subscribers will receive a free
1001 Dark Nights story
The First Night
by Lexi Blake & M.J. Rose

Discover 1001 Dark Nights Collection Four

Go to www.1001DarkNights.com for more information.

ROCK CHICK REAWAKENING by Kristen Ashley
A Rock Chick Novella

ADORING INK by Carrie Ann Ryan
A Montgomery Ink Novella

SWEET RIVALRY by K. Bromberg

SHADE'S LADY by Joanna Wylde
A Reapers MC Novella

RAZR by Larissa Ione
A Demonica Underworld Novella

ARRANGED by Lexi Blake
A Masters and Mercenaries Novella

TANGLED by Rebecca Zanetti
A Dark Protectors Novella

HOLD ME by J. Kenner
A Stark Ever After Novella

SOMEHOW, SOME WAY by Jennifer Probst
A Billionaire Builders Novella

TOO CLOSE TO CALL by Tessa Bailey
A Romancing the Clarksons Novella

HUNTED by Elisabeth Naughton
An Eternal Guardians Novella

EYES ON YOU by Laura Kaye
A Blasphemy Novella

BLADE by Alexandra Ivy/Laura Wright
A Bayou Heat Novella

DRAGON BURN by Donna Grant
A Dark Kings Novella

TRIPPED OUT by Lorelei James
A Blacktop Cowboys® Novella

STUD FINDER by Lauren Blakely

MIDNIGHT UNLEASHED by Lara Adrian
A Midnight Breed Novella

HALLOW BE THE HAUNT by Heather Graham
A Krewe of Hunters Novella

DIRTY FILTHY FIX by Laurelin Paige
A Fixed Novella

THE BED MATE by Kendall Ryan
A Room Mate Novella

NIGHT GAMES by CD Reiss
A Games Novella

NO RESERVATIONS by Kristen Proby
A Fusion Novella

DAWN OF SURRENDER by Liliana Hart
A MacKenzie Family Novella

Discover 1001 Dark Nights Collection One

Go to www.1001DarkNights.com for more information.

FOREVER WICKED by Shayla Black
CRIMSON TWILIGHT by Heather Graham
CAPTURED IN SURRENDER by Liliana Hart
SILENT BITE: A SCANGUARDS WEDDING by Tina Folsom
DUNGEON GAMES by Lexi Blake
AZAGOTH by Larissa Ione
NEED YOU NOW by Lisa Renee Jones
SHOW ME, BABY by Cherise Sinclair
ROPED IN by Lorelei James
TEMPTED BY MIDNIGHT by Lara Adrian
THE FLAME by Christopher Rice
CARESS OF DARKNESS by Julie Kenner

Also from 1001 Dark Nights

TAME ME by J. Kenner

Discover 1001 Dark Nights Collection Two

Go to www.1001DarkNights.com for more information.

WICKED WOLF by Carrie Ann Ryan
WHEN IRISH EYES ARE HAUNTING by Heather Graham
EASY WITH YOU by Kristen Proby
MASTER OF FREEDOM by Cherise Sinclair
CARESS OF PLEASURE by Julie Kenner
ADORED by Lexi Blake
HADES by Larissa Ione
RAVAGED by Elisabeth Naughton
DREAM OF YOU by Jennifer L. Armentrout
STRIPPED DOWN by Lorelei James
RAGE/KILLIAN by Alexandra Ivy/Laura Wright
DRAGON KING by Donna Grant
PURE WICKED by Shayla Black
HARD AS STEEL by Laura Kaye
STROKE OF MIDNIGHT by Lara Adrian
ALL HALLOWS EVE by Heather Graham
KISS THE FLAME by Christopher Rice
DARING HER LOVE by Melissa Foster
TEASED by Rebecca Zanetti
THE PROMISE OF SURRENDER by Liliana Hart

Also from 1001 Dark Nights

THE SURRENDER GATE By Christopher Rice
SERVICING THE TARGET By Cherise Sinclair

Discover 1001 Dark Nights Collection Three

Go to www.1001DarkNights.com for more information.

About Donna Grant

New York Times and USA Today bestselling author Donna Grant has been praised for her "totally addictive" and "unique and sensual" stories. She's the author of more than fifty novels spanning multiple genres of romance. Her latest acclaimed series, Dark Kings, features dragons, the Fae, and immortal Highlanders who are dark, dangerous, and irresistible.

She lives with her two children, three dogs, and four cats in Texas.

For more information about Donna, visit her website at www.DonnaGrant.com.

Discover More Donna Grant

Dragon King
A Dark Kings Novella
By Donna Grant

A Woman On A Mission

Grace Clark has always done things safe. She's never colored outside of the law, but she has a book due and has found the perfect spot to break through her writer's block. Or so she thinks. Right up until Arian suddenly appears and tries to force her away from the mountain. Unaware of the war she just stumbled into, Grace doesn't just discover the perfect place to write, she finds Arian - the most gorgeous, enticing, mysterious man she's ever met.

A King With a Purpose

Arian is a Dragon King who has slept away centuries in his cave. Recently woken, he's about to leave his mountain to join his brethren in a war when he's alerted that someone has crossed onto Dreagan. He's ready to fight...until he sees the woman. She's innocent and mortal - and she sets his blood aflame. He recognizes the danger approaching her just as the dragon within him demands he claim her for his own...

* * * *

Dragon Fever
A Dark Kings Novella
By Donna Grant

A yearning that won't be denied

Rachel Marek is a journalist with a plan. She intends to expose the truth about dragons to the world — and her target is within sight. Nothing matters but getting the truth, especially not the ruggedly handsome, roguishly thrilling Highlander who oozes danger and charm. And when she finds the truth that shatters her faith, she'll have to trust her heart to the very man who can crush it...

A legend in the flesh

Suave, dashing Asher is more than just a man. He's a Dragon King — a being who has roamed this planet since the beginning of time. With everything on the line, Asher must choose to trust an enemy in the form of an all too alluring woman whose tenacity and passion captivate him. Together, Asher and Rachel must fight for their lives — and their love — before an old enemy destroys them both...

Constantine: A History

Coming September 12, 2017 is a special short story all about our favorite King of Kings.
Read on for a preview
and be one of the first to pre-order!

* * * *

The 12th of August, human year 1601
Dreagan

As I write this, I cannot help but look back over the years. The date the mortals use means nothing to me, or any of the other Dragon Kings. Yet, we are bound by it, if we are to live in their world.

A world I helped to create.

A world my kind must now hide in.

I finished visiting those Dragon Kings who have chosen to sleep. It is a burden I gladly take on to give my brethren a chance to escape the hellish lives we have chosen to live. After all these untold thousands of years that rain around me like the stars above, it doesn't get any easier.

I soldier on, as do the other Kings. Because we hold out hope that one day we'll be able to bring our dragons home again.

Even as I impart the past decade of information to the sleeping Kings, I know there is one thought that never leaves them. When can they see their dragons again? *I wish I had an answer.*

But even as all of the magic on this realm flows through me, I have no solution.

V was the last Dragon King I saw. I sat beside him as he slept, but I could still feel his rage for what the humans had done to him. For V – and aye, even for Ulrik – the answer is simple. Show the mortals who we really are. Resume our rightful place as rulers of the realm with magic and might.

But how can I? After every King swore to protect the defenseless, magic-less mortals?

There is no remedy. Just as I feel the magic draining from this world, I wonder how long before we can remain hidden. Before we have no choice but to show the humans that dragons are a part of their world.

Before we're once more at war.

Though I will try and tell the mortals there is no weapon they have that can destroy us, I know they will not listen. Still, I will attempt to save them – even though I know the end result will be their demise.

There is no winning for either side, but especially not for us Dragon Kings. Not now, and I fear not ever.

Constantine, the King of Golds
King of Dragon Kings

On behalf of 1001 Dark Nights,

Liz Berry and M.J. Rose would like to thank ~

Steve Berry
Doug Scofield
Kim Guidroz
Jillian Stein
InkSlinger PR
Dan Slater
Asha Hossain
Chris Graham
Pamela Jamison
Fedora Chen
Kasi Alexander
Jessica Johns
Dylan Stockton
Richard Blake
BookTrib After Dark
and Simon Lipskar

Made in the USA
Middletown, DE
10 September 2017